ADVANCE PRAISE FOR *FORMS OF DEFIANCE*

Some writers work with hammers, some with shovels, still others with pitchforks or chainsaws. Cynthia Sample's tool of choice is the scalpel, an instrument she wields to thrilling, deliciously wicked effect in *Forms of Defiance*. Each story in this stellar collection aims true and cuts deep, laying open the essential inner workings of our all too human selves. Unnerving at times, and delightful all of the time, *Forms of Defiance* is a work of masterful literary dissection.

Ben Fountain, author of *Brief Encounters with Che Guevara*, *Billy Lynn's Long Halftime Walk*

Cynthia Sample's quirky and outrageously insightful stories sing with a voice so particular and peculiar that the reader can't help but be seduced. I was. One after another, story after story, Sample entertains us, all the while sneakily investigating and laying bare all the secrets of humanity. I've never read anything like these – and I only want more.

Robin Oliveira, author of *My Name is Mary Sutter*, *I Always Loved You*, *Winter Sisters*

In one of the stories in this stunning debut collection, Cynthia Croan Sample invokes the astronomical concept of parallax when describing a documentary her protagonist watches at an observatory: "The camera pulls back over and over again," she writes, "each time showing what the universe looks like from that imagined vantage point." *Forms of Defiance* gives us fifty-three parallactic views on another kind of universe, the universe of fears, desires, hopes, and secrets inside us all. Her book is brilliantly original, fiercely honest, and laced with a wise and heartbreaking wit. In short, it's the real thing: a book that truly matters. I urge you to read it and share it with those you love.

David Jauss, author of *Glossolalia: New & Selected Stories,*
Nice People: New & Selected Stories II

Forms of Defiance is a restless, eccentric, witty book of stories that defy definition. Some stories are shorter than their titles. One is a list of Bible verses. One is a prayer diary. One is an essay about coffins. One consists of a recorded tornado warning alert. Cynthia Sample defies form by borrowing forms. The results are astonishing—astringently ironic, yet intimate. She is a mistress of the killer one-liner. And at the heart of every character is a special kind of bravado in the face of what life throws at us.

Douglas Glover, Author, *Elle, Savage Love*

FORMS
OF
DEFIANCE

Stories

CYNTHIA C. SAMPLE

Attention schools and businesses: for discounted copies on large orders,
please contact the publisher directly. Books are brought to the trade by
Ingram.

For information contact:
Unsolicited Press
Portland, Oregon
www.unsolicitedpress.com
orders@unsolicitedpress.com
619-354-8005

Cover Design: Kathryn Gerhardt
Cover Image Credit: Susan Perkins
Editor: Bekah Stogner
ISBN: 978-1-950730-94-0

For Samantha Jane and Sally Anne

Too many words ...
are not needed by true elders.

Richard Rohr, *Falling Upward*

Contents

I.

LOVE

People All Around Are Looking

The Sound of My Love

MY HUSBAND'S SILENCE is mostly thin, the world inside our house still, except for the ongoing prattle of Fox commentators on the state of the economy. Sometimes though, my husband's silence thickens like a choking smoke: when he can't find his keys or the television is on the fritz or his computer is having a conniption fit. Even if curses come out of his mouth, he remains poker-faced, which, after all, is a form of silence. It takes an expert to discern what he really means, what intentions lie under the surface of the stoic muscles holding his cheeks immobile and his forehead expressionless. It requires exquisite attention to know if the air is thin or thick, if the house is safe or dangerous, if he will come to me or no.

On the Occasions that Lula Sought an Answer from Her Mother's Bible Concordance

DANCE (danced, dancing)

Ecc	3:4	a time to *d* and a time to mourn
2Sa	6:14	*d* before the Lord
Ps	30:11	You turned my waiting into *d*

LUST (lusted, lusts)

Pr	6:25	Do not *l* in your heart
1Th	4:5	not in passionate *l* like the heathen
1PE	4:3	in debauchery, *l*, drunkenness

LOVE (beloved, loved, lovely, lover, lover's, lovers, loves, loving, loving-kindness)

Ge	20:13	'This is how you can show you *l*
	22:2	your only son, Isaac, who you *l*
Jos	22:5	careful to *l* the Lord your God

ADULTERY (adulterers, adulteress, adulteries)

Lev	20:10	both the *a* and the adulteress must
Heb	13:14	for God will judge the *a*
Hos	3:1	she is loved by another and is an *a*
Jer	3:8	sent her away because of all her *a*
Ex	20:14	You shall not commit *a*

Mt	5:32	The divorced woman commits *a*
Mk	10:11	marries another woman commits *a*
Jn	8:4	woman was caught in the act of *a*

DIVORCE (divorced, divorces)

Dt	22:19	He must not *d* her as long as he lives
Dt.	24:1	and writes her a certificate of *d*
Mal	2:16	"I hate *d*," says the Lord God
Mt	19:3	for a man to *d* his wife for any reason
1Co	7:27	Are you married? Do not seek a *d*

LOVE (beloved, loved, lovely, lover, lover's, lovers, loves, loving, loving-kindness)

| Jdg1 | 4:16 | You hate me! You don't really *l* me |

LIE (liar, liars lied, lies lying)

Lev	19:11	Do not *l*
Nu	23:19	God is not a man that he should *l*
1Jn	2:21	because no *l* comes from the truth
Ac	5:4	You have not *l* to men but to God

END (ends)

Ps	119:112	to the very *e*
Ps	1:19	such is the *e* of all who go
Ps	5:4	but in the *e* she is bitter as gall
Ps	14:13	and joy may *e* in grief
Ps	16:25	in the *e* it leads to death

Ps   19:20   and in the *e* you will be wise

FORGIVE (forgiveness, forgave, forgives, forgiving)
    Ge   50:17   I ask you to *f* your brothers the sins
    Ex   10:17   He will not *f* your rebellion
    Isa   15:25   *f* my sin and come back with me
    Col   1:14   in whom we have redemption the *f*
    Eph   4:32   to one another, *f* each other

SECRET (secrets, secretly)
    Dt   29:29   the *s* things belong
    Ps   90:8   our *s* sins in the light
    Pr   21:14   a gift given in *s* soothes anger
    Jer   23:24   Can anyone hide in *s* places?
    Mk   4:11   the *s* of the kingdom
    Php   4:12   I have learned the *s*

Proof

YOU MEET HIM at one of those cocktail parties held on top of a building in a loft in which lots of windows overlook Dallas. It's 1980, and everyone here that isn't smoking grass is drinking white wine. All of the young women are wearing silk miniskirts if we've had time to change, or else business suits with tiny bows at our collar, instead of ties; we do this because we're feminists who just got off work. A lot of us aren't married yet. We're thirty and we're nervous.

You are introduced into a little knot of people, including one athletic-looking Stephen, who holds the little knot enthralled with hilarity. A gorgeous set of twins sandwich him: a woman with big breasts and strong legs, and her equally gorgeous brother, who is sure to be a tennis pro or a stockbroker. Jokes become increasingly sexual until Stephen tells one about a threesome in Italy. He looks at you the whole time, as if this last joke was meant specially for you. You throw back your head and guffaw. Afterwards you wonder if the way you laugh was feminine enough for such a catch as he. You wonder a bit about the twins and the joke and whether he asked for your number from the hostess.

He calls. Predictably, he owns a convertible, a rust colored Fiat. The twins are cramped into the tiny black backseat. The restaurant is in a seedy part of town, where the prostitutes cruise, but it's the best Tex-Mex in town, and you feel safe: two men after all. You laugh some, but not as often or as loud as the first time you met. It occurs to you that the twins might always date each other, feel a little titillation at the thought, but you dismiss luridness. That kind of thing doesn't occur except in soap operas.

Stephen doesn't push you for sex before marriage. Instead, you neck and pet and fantasize over the phone. The twins are the wedding attendants, and parents are jubilant that, finally, their children are settled. On your honeymoon, Stephen makes love to you every other morning. He calls the twins every day from the hotel in Mexico. At home, they meet the plane, and in the Fiat, drive you to your apartment.

Routine sets in. Stephen works at Republic Bank, analyzing debts, and you work at Fair Abstract and Title, studying heavy plat books to prove that people will own what they pay for. Stephen insists on buying a house in the best part of town, but you don't fight the decision: the house is ivy-covered and has a fenced back yard with a swing set. The twins start to irritate you, and when the girl-twin gets married, you're glad for the relief. You arrange dates for the boy-twin but nothing works out. One date asks if the boy-twin suffers post-traumatic stress or something because he was so erratic the whole night.

Sex settles into habit, once every three weeks. You're thirty-five and starting to panic. The fertility specialist talks to Stephen alone. This makes you nervous because Stephen storms out of the doctor's office and refuses to return. You call the doctor to ask why, but he doesn't return your calls. Then, as if God saw you tossing and turning at night, a miracle happens: you conceive. The baby-girl is born perfect and you rejoice.

Parental demands are more taxing than you could have ever expected; returning to Fair Title loses its appeal. Stephen is now necessary in additional ways. The boy-twin attends all family functions and Stephen insists on his being your precious baby-girl's godfather. "He'll protect her. Know what I mean?" Stephen says this with a Marlon Brando accent then tweaks your breast. You cannot imagine why you laugh along with him. You remember the joke about Italy, and the intimate glance Stephen still gives you occasionally. At the christening, the boy-twin shows up with an engraved silver cup, vintage lace dresses, and Madame Alexander dolls.

Time passes. So fascinating is your baby-girl's development, you hardly notice that you initiate lovemaking more and more of the time. Stephen and the boy-twin take up kayaking, and take weekend trips on rivers you never see. When they return, Stephen doesn't kiss you before he reads the mail.

You ask him to stop going out of town. Baby-girl needs him: time not money. "Can't you find a hobby for all of us?" you suggest. Stephen looks at you quizzically. "Give up the boating," you repeat and you hear a dependent voice you would have deplored not even a year ago. Stephen replies, "Don't be ridiculous." The next time, you beg with a reddened face. "Why?" Stephen demands. You cannot bring yourself to answer. Finally, you insist. "Don't do this," Stephen replies, and heads to the garage to clean the kayak. He doesn't touch you for months, but continues to tickle baby-girl's feet and take her to the park most nights while you do the dishes.

In the dark, when you find the courage, you reach for him. You stroke his face, his arms, his hips, and his penis. Finally, he turns you over and rocks till he comes. When he leaves your body, he slaps you on the hips and says: "Thank you ma'am," and laughs his golden laugh. As if nothing untoward had ever happened.

You turn your head into the pillow, fist the hem of the pillowcase.

With proof.

Forms of Defiance 1:
Inane Promises Made to the Listener/Reader/Other Ignored, Broken, or Abandoned But Which Evidently Are Irrelevant to the Course of Life

The Rule: Be nice.

The Defiance: Oops.

Windows

I'LL START. BILL won't help, though he promised. When I first saw this place, I complained at the filth, the dingy light, despite the huge windows. Bill protested that he'd clean the damn windows himself, for God's sake. But of course, being Bill, he did not. So I'll start; being clean on one side is better than nothing I guess. I'm the one that can't stand them a second longer. I'd like to enjoy the view just once from a comfortable position. The scene is beautiful from the deck: the red-streaked bluff, the running river so clear that, if you squint, the green river bottom can be seen underneath the reflection of the bank on the other side.

Tol, our lawyer, built this place after his divorce, handed over napkin-ideas to some local contractor. "Make a man's place," he told the guy, "a solitary place." Now Tol's bought property around the bend. Now he wants a house big enough for his kids to come, and he sold this place to my husband. Tol evidently never cleaned it, or fixed it up. He just came up here to fish or sit and drink: defiance, I suppose. Bill came alone too for a while. I wasn't asked along until now.

It's part of the marital drift, the sum of a million little disconnects. The myriad irritations, seemingly inconsequential in and of themselves, that morphed finally into a rage at life in general: nothing turned out like you'd dreamed. Although your love started out bursting with the hope that *your* marriage would be different. That *your* intimacy would expand and not contract into nothingness like the end of old movies. That *your* romance would remain central to your being, instead of only remembered or felt at the end – at the funeral of whoever left first.

We're here for only a week. Our kids, grown with families of their own and no longer the glue between Bill and me, say we need to "bond" again. So, to give our marriage one last try, we drove up here on the frantic interstate through the poverty of south Arkansas, and up into the Ozarks. Our mouths silent, golden-oldies bridging the gap between us, softening the edges of the encasement in ourselves. Our first night, the fans whir against the chirping of the birds, and our first morning, I wake to Bill already on the river. And the place is filthy.

Coffee, reading, a buttery scone. I see him standing in the water, his rod casting and casting the fly. Even if he were closer, I wouldn't be able to make out his features, because the windows are almost opaque.

I pull out the cleaning supplies, start on the kitchen. In a couple of hours, my hands are rough with the cleaners, and I rest for a sweaty minute. No Bill, but the place is better. Still, the dirty windows rankle. I purse my lips as I watch him, casting and casting and casting. I imagine his mind void of me, and ignoring the state of this place.

So I'll start. There's vinegar, and a stack of old newspapers. I pull up a chair and climb up to reach the upper windows that overlook the river. I go back and forth, inside and out, to clean the few windows without screens, the ones I can reach. In an hour, I've done what I can do alone. Bill swore he'd clean everything when he bought the place. Of course, he put it off and now it's left to me. My victim voice whines even to my own ears as I hear a "whoop-de-do" from the river; the fish are biting for him.

I sit down, with nothing else I can do alone. If the grime were only on one side, I could get them clear without any help. I try to distract myself with the novel I've brought. A philosophical book, a literary book, well suited to my interests, nothing at all Bill would read. Whenever I look up, obsession with the remaining grime niggles; it takes more and more effort to set the feeling aside and return to the book. Why the hell doesn't he do something? Instead, he's down there, throwing a string out into the water, over and over again. Alone, only nodding, still silent, water waist deep, probably freezing his ass off.

Finally, he trudges back up to the cabin, holding the line of fish in one hand and the fly rod in the other. He strips off the waders, wipes his feet, cleans the trout he caught. "I got started," I say. "I already did the inside." His eyebrows become quizzical. "Oh. Yeah," he answers. I keep my own counsel until lunch. Holding my tongue is easy these days. After we eat, without prompting and to my surprise, he says, "I'll get the ladder." We fuss about how the windows should be cleaned. I want him to squeegee them, then wipe them down with the vinegar and newspapers. He says it's enough to hose them off, but deposits the other supplies in a blue plastic bucket and hooks it to the ladder. I keep my mouth shut and think: he'll never get them clean without the vinegar.

"Great," I think to reply, and set to shelf-papering the kitchen cabinets, which I do instead of reading my novel because I feel guilty reading while he works. The cabin is so small and he watches me inside, knocks on the glass.

"Hand me more paper towels," he says, and I bite my tongue, accommodate him. I see streaks after he finishes with the squeegee and begins to wipe with the vinegar. "You missed a spot," I say. Suddenly I realize he can't see where the smudges are because he's outside. I pull up the chair, and point to where the smudges remain. He wipes again. I can tell he's concentrating; he doesn't look me in the eyes. The smudge remains and I realize I missed the spot on my side. I grab a rag and wipe again.

I go back to the shelf paper, but the scenario repeats itself over and over: he wipes, I point, he wipes again, but I need to wipe my side again. Some spots won't come off at all. A scraper, Bill says, is necessary for them, a glue or something when the cabin was built. Finally, we cease snipping "it's on your side," and just point, wipe, point, then wipe again in little motions that get the job done.

Bill grills the trout; I set the little oval table in the corner with two places and make a salad. After we eat, we sit on the couch and face the windows. The screens are open and the breeze comes through, cool and free of the city toxins. We watch the river as if we were outside in the wild. Listen to the river silence without a television pulling our attention to an abstract set of facts that have little to do with us. We can hear the bob-white males calling, and Bill takes my left hand, gently, his square, rough finger around my palm. With his other hand, he points to the window in front of us. "We missed some spots," he says.

"It's good enough," I answer. "Look there." I point with my right hand at a woodpecker, just hammering away at the tree outside.

Extol Him Who Rides on the Clouds

Call me Magdalene.
Not Maggie. Not Meg. And certainly not Dolly, for God's
    sake.
Call me Magdalene. Let the syllables roll off your tongue.
    Slowly... slowly...

Let the connotation seep into your stomach, your very skeleton,
    your middle there.
Take a breath. Narrow your eyes. What do you want?

Think: do you *really* love your life? Your job ... your grown
    children ... your spouse?
Is what you have now really enough for you?
Take another breath.

Touch my cheek ... my silver-sheathed breast ... me.
Keep breathing now.

Hear the raging air blowing all around us. Feel the wind's
    unpredictability.
Sense the precipice beneath our toes. Smell the gift.
See how our bodies sway just before they're beyond choice?
How our chests cease to heave?

We fly for an instant, holding each other for an infinite
moment of understanding.
See the puffs of dust rise in frilly clouds that our bones make
as they crack on the sun-scorched earth.

The Complaint

Dear Mr. Mike Fleiss:

My grandson looked up on the Internet and found out that you are the producer of The Bachelor, The Bachelorette and also Bachelor in Paradise. I have a few things to say but I won't address BIP since my mother taught me to ignore bad manners and that show is definitely bad manners, despite everyone watching it while eating chips and drinking wine even though they won't admit it.

First of all: this is not a complaint letter. It's a fan letter, but with suggestions for your franchise. Bachelor Nation is successful, but it could be more successful.

During Sean's season, you had a grandmother drive up in a limo with her granddaughter. Now it makes entirely good sense to introduce your granddaughter to such a nice boy as that Sean, who clearly isn't on the make, as we used to call it.

My question for you is: what about the grandmother??? She didn't look married to me, and do you REALIZE how many grandparents are out there who are looking for love? I remind you that WE are the baby boomers and that husbands die earlier than their wives. We even have our own organization: AARP. They accept advertising! You are missing a major opportunity.

I really am incensed that all these girls are in their 20s. These girls do not need help. The more mature women, like myself, who have lost or ditched our husbands, are the ones who would be there for the "right reasons" and who would "listen to our hearts." These young people cannot possibly know their own minds at their age, like we do, because we have seen the trials of life.

What you definitely need to do is start The Bachelorette for older women. For one thing, most of us are NOT going to go on those Internet dating sites. One of my church friends did it and wound up with a psychopath. You could call your show: The Bachelorette-A.

It may be hard to find twenty-five breathing 65+ year old men with enough money to travel to casting. Yet that fact alone would help the Bachelorette-A choose, because, as anyone knows, no woman in her right mind wants a man who can't afford an occasional trip. Now you could have trouble finding two, let alone twenty-five, suitable men for Bachelorette-A that have the kind of abs you all seem to be obsessed with. Please do not concern yourself: we are not obsessed with muscles anymore. A beer gut of over 20 lbs., however, might be a deal-breaker. Perhaps not, though; you could hand out those Spanx-like belts sold on Home Shopping Network. Maybe you could even get a quantity discount.

Forget any worries about bald heads. None of us have an issue with that at our age. You know what they say about bald heads and prowess. Ha Ha!

One thing you need to watch out when choosing women for the Bachelorette-A are those facelifts. I'm not at all sure those would photograph well on television judging from the movie stars. Plus, those duck-lips are definitely out. Despite how tempting it is to fix your face, when you take off your clothes, you're in major trouble if your age spots sprinkle your stomach or you've ever had a weight gain. Your skin just looks like wrinkled sandpaper. You wouldn't want anyone leaving after the Fantasy Suite claiming he'd been bamboozled.

Speaking of appropriate attire, the Bachelorette-A ought to be allowed to wear sleeves at all times. If she goes on any of those beach dates, she wouldn't want her arms flapping in the wind like a surrender flag.

Plus ... and this is <u>critical</u>. Every season you make someone rappel down an office building, then smooch halfway down. None of us will do it because in that harness, our ass would look like a sack full of potatoes. Plus, there's just every reason to think that some man will have a heart attack halfway down, ruining everything.

Be sure to include some good dancing. And I don't mean that hugging to the tune of a band getting free advertising out in the middle of some piazza in Italy. I'm talking about the real thing: either Rock and Roll or a Big Band. It's been said that dancing is laughing in the face of death. Most women want a man who can dance.

Now you have to be careful about people's children. No contestant should be allowed to meet anyone's kids until <u>after</u> the Fantasy Suite. Most of us need all the help we can on that score. Though we love them to death, our kids and their opinions, especially with all that eye-rolling, can really get in the way of letting go. Plus, Chris Harrison should be instructed to lecture the contestants on remembering they are choosing and being chosen for themselves, not for those kids. Most of that kind of thing can be worked out unless someone's a gold digger. You probably will need a lawyer for that part.

Another benefit of The Bachelorette-A is that it would flummox Reality Steve. I've watched him on the Internet and he looks about thirty himself. He has consistently spoiled the results on all your versions of Find Love the Easy Way Through Television, but he won't have a <u>clue</u> how to predict what <u>we</u> will do.

These are my ideas for your NEW SHOW and I offer myself as a candidate for the first Bachelorette-A. I am as good-looking as anyone could expect at my age, and I'm not looking for health insurance. I'm just looking for love, like everyone else.

Yours very sincerely,

Lula

P.S. You might want to shorten the number of episodes. For one thing, people get tired flying all over the world like that. Plus, at our age you never know what'll happen.

Regular Theft
or
The Playlist that Donnie Presented to Cecilia as a Parting Gift on the Steps of Abbott Hall in Austin, Texas

1. "Feelin' Groovy" by Simon & Garfunkel
2. "Blowin' in the Wind" by Bob Dylan

3. "I Want to Hold Your Hand" by The Beatles
4. "Cecilia" by Simon & Garfunkel

5. "Like a Rolling Stone" by Bob Dylan
6. "(I Can't Get No) Satisfaction" by The Rolling Stones
7. "Ice" by Sarah McLachlan

8. "Hold On …. This is Gonna Hurt Like Hell" by Sarah McLachlan
9. "It Ain't Me Babe" by Bob Dylan

Dr. Pepper with Lime

JUDITH *WANTED* THE necklace, that's all. She'd seen it on her grandmother, and then on Aunt Sallie, although never on her own mother. Judith simply wanted it for herself and knew it was meant for her instead of her cousin, whatever the rules of property. Just last night, as she planned her escape during dinner, she'd watched Aunt Sallie finger it, then unclasp it on the way up the stairs after they ate. Judith knew that once Aunt Sallie and Uncle Jepthah were in in their bedroom, with the door closed behind them, the necklace would be laid in the jewelry box and the chest's drawer—the top one—would be shut.

That necklace deserved better. Aunt Sallie allowed it on her mottled crepe neck amid those voile blouses tucked into shapeless skirts. She might have just as well worn a housedress. Ridiculous.

Judith took it. Quietly, on her last day before the train home to McFall. Judith was packed, her worn leather suitcase all strapped up, waiting for her by the door at the bottom of the staircase. She slipped the jewelry around her neck, fastened it as to hang as low as possible, and buttoned her cardigan all the way.

Judith planned to walk to the bus stop by herself. "You know how I hate good-byes, a lot of fussy kissing and all," she had claimed when the plans were set. Aunt Sallie and Uncle Jepthah were in the parlor waiting to wave good-bye, as respectful of her wishes as pie after dinner.

Judith walked down the stairs, heard the second one creak. She wiggled her fingers and smiled at her aunt and uncle, headed for Miller's Pharmacy and Thomas Hayden. The suitcase wasn't heavy. Her annual trip from McFall to St. Jo lasted half the summer. She owned few things anyway and she'd brought most of what she cared about, but the case was light. She stopped at the end of the street as soon as she turned the corner, and unbuttoned the sweater so the sapphire would glint in the sun. It matched her eyes. When her science class studied rocks last year, her classmates said her eyes were the color of poisonous chalcanthite. At the time, she'd been bothered, but she'd gotten used to the idea. Sapphire was close enough.

Dr. Hayden was thirty-two with a wife, a child and a medical practice. He was so successful, it was said he carried five hundred dollars cash in his wallet. His wife, Doris, had let herself grow fat since their baby and was interested in nothing much. Unlike Judith with her sapphire and platinum dangle. Unlike Judith who was interested in everything that had wit, complications or adventure, not the least of which was Dr. Hayden.

"Dr. Pepper with lime, Mrs. Miller," she said over the vinyl seat and handed fifty cents to her. It was very important to pay her own way.

Dr. Hayden slipped into the booth opposite, looking over his shoulder as he did.

"What'll it be, Tom?" Mrs. Miller said. "How's that new baby?"

"Oh, Billy's a real doll, Wilma. Thanks. In fact, Judith here is interviewing to be his babysitter, aren't you Judith?"

Mrs. Miller looked pointedly at the leather suitcase next to the table.

"I'll have coffee, Wilma. Sugar."

Mrs. Miller brought the coffee, set the sugar bowl down next to the cup with its protruding spoon. Dr. Hayden leaned over the table, his forearms around his coffee. "Graduation present?" He touched the sapphire in the necklace. "Matches your eyes."

Judith laughed a bit and nodded. She cocked her head, smiled prettily, and fingered the necklace. "Oh, Dr. Hayden!"

"Don't you think you should call me Thomas now?"

Judith sipped her Dr. Pepper. The lime made it tingle on her lips, almost like a little bite, even through the red lipstick. "I suppose I should," she said. "Thomas."

Over his shoulder, Judith saw Lucy Jordan walking toward them. Lucy Jordan couldn't seem to get to them soon enough. "Hi, Dr. Hayden. Judith." She leaned forward as if to sit down, but looked, and noticed the suitcase, but immediately Judith scooted toward the edge of the seat. Lucy stood up straight again. "I got a letter from my big sister over in McFall, Judith. She said you'd won the Lincoln Award at school last year. Congratulations."

The Lincoln Award was always Judith's since her essays were always the best. Like "Margery Goes to Town," about Margery Fetta's race to the hospital to have her baby, in which Judith compared the woman's contractions to a car out of control. Then there was "Casey Catches the Train," about Teddy Smith's trip to St. Louis for the World's Fair. She'd lied in "Cheese Makes the Heart Grow Fonder," about her mother's house party when Aunt Sallie visited McFall the summer of Judith's sophomore year; in that one, she made fun of Aunt Sallie's obsession with her mother's cheese straws. Why should Lucy care? "Thanks," she said to Lucy and hoped her curt tone would dismiss the chatterbox.

Lucy turned around, headed for Mr. Miller behind the pharmacy counter. She stopped, turned, and said, "Pretty necklace Judith." This worried Judith a bit, but she took solace in the fact that Aunt Sallie hated scandal.

Three hours later Judith was showering at the Three Creeks Resort and Motel outside St. Jo. Dr. Hayden was dead asleep in one of the two beds, his blond head on naked, crossed arms under the soft light. Judith walked back into the dim room with a towel around her and the sapphire necklace sparkling between her breasts. She began to dress.

She donned her traveling suit and reached for the phone on the table between the beds to call a cab. Fortunately, the cord was long enough for her to turn her back to Dr. Hayden. She kept her voice low although that wasn't very difficult; her adrenaline wasn't racing at all and she was only half concerned he'd wake.

Judith felt not a sliver of remorse. Aunt Sallie had plenty of jewelry and wouldn't miss this; anybody in this situation would be too embarrassed to admit what had happened. Doris Hayden had a nice house, plenty of security, and lots of friends. Even if Dr. Hayden was caught, Doris would forgive him and their life would go back to normal, only Doris Hayden would have a lot more power now.

She, Judith Hunsuch, would get herself a bus ticket to Dallas and start her new life. She could buy that ticket for one hundred dollars; she had already checked. With the $30 in her pocketbook from home to get back to McFall and the five hundred dollars Dr. Hayden kept in his wallet, there would be plenty left over to get herself settled. Judith was going to escape them all. She'd start over and never have to avoid anyone again. Her Lincoln Awards would more than impress and get her a decent job in a decent-sized city. Away where decent and more exciting men lived. Away where there was more happiness to be had. Away from Missouri, her boring relatives and the promised college life her parents had withdrawn: at the very last minute when she had no options.

Dr. Hayden didn't stir. Men were predictable, she thought. He's just like Pop or Uncle Jepthah or the stupid boys in McFall. They all collapsed and she was left wide-eyed, staring, bored.

She looked around the room to verify she hadn't forgotten anything, patted the top of her jacket where the necklace was secreted underneath. She rifled through Dr. Hayden's clothes. He'd left them in a hurried pile with his pants on the bottom but she had little trouble finding the tri-fold wallet in his back pocket. She flipped the wallet open and as she did, thought it spread like legs willing to trade. She smiled at the unbidden sentence in her mind. She was quite good at metaphor; hence the Lincoln Award. She stared into the leather V-shape in her hands. A one-dollar bill, not even crisp. Two Dr. Peppers with lime. Tingles. Then bites.

The Prayer Diary of Doreen Newton

MONDAY

Dear God,

Pastor says we should build up our faith by writing out our prayers and their answers. I doubt it'll do much good. Mostly since Harry died, all the answers seem to be NO! But that's what Pastor says, so here goes, God.

First of all, the garage door has warped some more. You of all people—well You're not a *people* I don't guess, but anyway—You ought to know I can't afford a contractor. So I'm asking You right now: how do I fix my garage door for $100?

Hmm . . . Hmm . . . Hmm . . .

So now I think You want me to call Richard. Harry hired him to build the storage room and Richard needed the money. Maybe he can fix it.

TUESDAY

Dear God,

I wish Richard would stop all that noise—every time another one of those boards falls down, I near 'bout jump out of my stockings.

But God, You're getting my garage fixed. Now, if You could make everyone stay home while I drive to the bank for the money to pay Richard, I'd really appreciate it. I can't lose my license what with Harry gone and all.

LATER

Dear God,

Help! Richard just said he's been thinking about me ever since his Esther died. He's asking to come over here for a decent meal, said he hasn't had one since Esther and her kitchen went their separate ways. He does look pretty thin. On TV yesterday, there was that story about Mother Teresa. Are You sending me a sign?

Now I'm having an idea and I'll bet it's from You. I'll cook him up something and just send it on home with him. Things have changed: men expect things of you when you have a date nowadays. I'll fix up some chicken and dumplings; that'll keep 'til he gets home.

WEDNESDAY

Dear God,

What'll I do now? Richard called up to thank me for the chicken and dumplings. Now he says he loves me. "Well, you're welcome," I said. But then he said it again, only louder. He wants to come on over here tonight. I didn't know *what* to say, so I answered: "Well, all right."

God, help me out of this!! I couldn't say, "Richard, I don't love *you*," so soon after Esther just died. That could hurt his feelings. I wouldn't know what to say to a man that wasn't Harry. Alone, I mean.

You stopped the traffic when I went to the bank yesterday. Now You gotta fix this! I pray that he NOT—I repeat NOT — come over here.

38

LATER

God,

Richard called to say his car won't start. "Guess our little date will just have to wait, honey." He actually called me 'honey', which Harry never did. Anyway, thank you that Richard isn't coming over here—and I do hope he gets his car fixed eventually.

Speaking of Harry, God—I hope You bless him wherever he is in heaven. Be sure to give him something to do—You know he always got bored; we always had that in common. And don't let him know about Richard. I'd hate to spoil things for Harry even the slightest little bit. You know Harry always was the jealous type. Why, I remember . . . well, God, You probably remember too, although I'll bet it doesn't make You blush.

So here's my prayer. Keep this pie from tipping over on the floorboard while I get it over to Richard's. I'll put it on his porch and just ring the bell. Even my mama didn't insist on a chaperone in broad daylight on the street. I don't want Richard to feel bad, God. I just don't want him calling me honey and coming over here.

THURSDAY

Dear God,

Who'd have thought, with that run-down shack, that Richard could get his car fixed in ONE DAY. He said he prayed about it, but I don't believe him. No one could live in that mess and be a praying person. Am I just being judgmental? Maybe his wife did everything and he's just . . . well, you know, stupid about real life, like most men. Even Harry, bless his heart.

Here's the reason for this prayer, God: Richard called first thing this morning and he wants to come over today. God, you've got to get me out of this. But don't—I repeat, DON'T—let anything happen to his car again. He can't afford it.

LATER

Here I am again, God. You HAVE to stop doing things to Richard. I didn't want him to fall off his porch, to get *hurt*. Heal that sprained foot as quick as possible cause he has to work. But DON'T let him come over here. Just don't let anything else bad happen to him.

FRIDAY

God, I haven't heard from Richard, and here it is noon already. Should I call over there? Just tell me what to do and I'll do it. Except I must be honest, at least with You. I don't want him to call me honey—not only because of Harry, but because yesterday, I remembered those dirty old men back in the '50s, always calling us young women 'honey', and 'sweet-kins'. Burns me up to think about that, even now. Why, like I was a child or a loose woman or something.

LATER

Dear God,

Pastor better not expect me to read this prayer journal out loud in Sunday School, because God, you know I *cannot* do that. Especially not after what happened tonight.

I don't know what came over me, God. Pastor says when we put things on paper, we figure them out (sort of like naming our sins). So here goes: when I took that beef stew and that praline cheesecake over to Richard, I only wanted to cheer him up. When I cleaned up his house, it was just because he was hurt and all. And when I overpaid him for fixing my garage door, I was just remembering that it's not easy making your dollars match your hours. I decided it was more important to help out than to have a chaperone. It was like an *executive* decision.

Maybe I should ask you to forgive me, or maybe I shouldn't. I just don't know. All I really wanted was to get my garage door fixed. Now I have to hide things from Pastor cause when Richard lifted his chin and yelled, "Cock-a-doodle-do!" as if he was about to get . . . well, You of all people ought to know. Why, I've plumb had the shivers ever since.

Richard didn't call me honey after I asked him not to. I guess that's an answer to prayer.

A Telling Phrase if Ever There Was One:
Juliet's Exercise in Convergence

JULIET'S HUSBAND OF thirty years receives a diagnosis: bone cancer. Juliet overhears this because, being a faithful wife, she is sitting next to her husband in the doctor's office. "This is going to hurt, isn't it?" her husband asks the doctor. When her husband grimaces at the answer, she stops breathing for some seconds.

Juliet normally tries to be a good Christian and so, despite her many character defects, she excuses herself and leaves the room. She kneels on the slick bathroom tile and prays for help from a God she feels she scarcely knows. After all, what with taking care of her family, she hasn't had much opportunity to understand religion and, anyway, she sometimes hates her husband, an impulse that seems contradictory to Jesus' teaching.

But today her desperation leads her to a straightforward, unencumbered plea for help. Yet she finds she cannot ask for deliverance or even a miracle. This could be because she sometimes hates her husband and sometimes even wants a miraculous deliverance from him into another life. Or it could be because she trusts God's help will come in the form best for everyone concerned: a matter of trust that God is nice instead of mean. Her discomfort with this double-edged prayer frustrates her and haunts her over the ensuing months. Still, both motivations seem true to her.

Juliet reports regularly via email to the many people who want access to her husband's suffering. This protects her sanity and also offers time for her to reflect on the previous decades.

Their computer is in a room separate from where he is dying so her recriminations and regrets and tears can remain a secret that doesn't add to his pain. She tries to pray but her doubts and guilts niggle her, vague and unreasonable impediments to peace.

When Juliet gets back into the limousine after the funeral, the radio blasts the last two lines of "A Matter of Trust" in which Billy Joel insists, "It's always been a matter of trust!" Although the car is evidently soundproof, the driver quickly flips the button to mute the song. But Juliet takes this as a sign from God although she didn't hear the whole song. A deep relief covers her like a blanketing answer to her pleas for help but without any clarity about herself. Because of hearing the song at just that particular moment, and especially the word 'always', she gives herself the benefit of the doubt.

That night Juliet sleeps like the dead, a telling phrase if ever there was one, because the caregiving was so demanding and lasted so long. The time was not near long enough for her, but she wouldn't have added a second to his suffering. At the same time, she wishes she wasn't alone in such a big bed, even though she dreams.

Plumage

ON FRIDAY, LULA finds herself lonelier than she can bear. So after wrestling her moral compass to the ground, she dresses, all the while wondering what alleviation she could possibly find at a bar catering to thirty-year-olds.

Still, Lula strips off her suit and showers, running the hot washcloth over her cobbled fleshy arms and her papery neck. Crepe paper is supposed to be a light-hearted thing, but her skin is colorless save for the brownish age speckles. As a defense against impulsive and humiliating sex, Lula neglects to shave her legs or the pubic hair the young women wax away nowadays. This she saw in a TV infomercial. She slathers her skin with an expensive, young-scented cream. She skips her diamond bracelet in favor of a beaded one.

She pulls on a tight undergarment meant to smooth out her mid-section cellulite, erase the lumps that are the reward of borne children and too many anti-depressant carbs. She rolls on silk stockings but then takes them off again because her adult daughter insists they date her like almost nothing else could. She echoes her daughter to herself: You need to try.

She applies makeup carefully: a thick cream for coverage, an iridescent white to her lids, and a heavy black line above her lashes – a cat-eye she saw in a magazine.

Her heels click on the tile as she leaves her apartment. They're old shoes, not sexy at all, with a rounded toe, but she doesn't teeter in them.

At the bar, she makes sure to sit so the candlelight from the tables illuminates her face, softening the years she was unable to hide. She orders a pricey Chardonnay off the menu and caresses the glass gingerly by the stem so as to hold in the chill. She might be lonely, but she isn't broke: despite the unfashionable shoes, despite the costume jewelry. She whispers under her breath: Money hasn't helped me so far.

A tall blonde leans against the bar at the other end. Her blouse is a gauzy voile that would cause most onlookers to miss the muscular arms; her silk pants barely reach her instep. Both wrists are bangled almost to her elbow, over the voile. One hand cradles an old-fashioned. The blonde hair is clearly a wig.

A man sits on the stool next to her, and slicks his white hair. He palms the bar, orders the house red, and takes no notice of Lula. He raises the deep garnet wine to his full lips and yellow teeth show as he begins to sip. He is about her own age, but he studies the gyrating girls on the little dance floor ten feet away.

Lula thinks young women look like children in dress-up clothes, their smooth faces glistening with sweat and their bodies peacock'd in finery they don't need yet. Even the boys are all still flat-stomached with strong legs. No teetering for them. Probably no loneliness either. Just young-adult angst and shallow moral conflicts about nothing in particular. Unaware, even, of the competition that is sure to define almost everything today and to come.

Lula catches the eye of one of the boys. As he walks toward her, she smiles but she feels like she's smiling at her daughter's boyfriend and notices he's squinting a bit as he approaches. She remembers: "You've got to try Mom," and silently talks to herself again: Just adorn yourself for the rivalry of the present night ahead. Hide from yourself the erosion of the years and the ever-diminishing value of your flesh. But go ahead: show your red feathers in the best light possible. Invite someone, anyone, into your space. Borrow their energy, their meaning, their life.

Try.
Try to care.

The Ditty

Girl regularly stomped her foot.
Then a ditty from her grandmother
presaged the future of women of another generation,
              but then maybe it was just her.
       'Greedy-gut, greedy-gut
       eat the whole world up
       and then ask for more.'

First, Girl demanded more Hershey's kisses,
        then more kisses from her beaus and
        then lots more kisses from that particular one.
            Surely she would be happy with that.
      Now she had a lifetime of kisses before her.

Unsatisfied, a last kiss was offered her.
        He was dying
        and she was greedy for more.

Special

LULA WAS PRETTY sure she was special but she was also pretty sure that she was not.

For one thing, she kept having great intentions. Even as a child, she would decide: make perfect grades, take a shower every morning, never talk in class again, turn her homework in on time, never gossip again about her supposed-friend Vicki, tell the priest the truth during confession. Anything to escape mediocrity, being average, like everyone else. But after she finally got to sleep and then woke up again, her life would proceed to fall completely apart once again.

These intentions kept recurring throughout her childhood when her mom turned off her bedroom light, then continued as Lula's adulthood unfolded, every night when she got the room dark enough to sleep after a long day of failure and/or procrastination. Yet with the good intentions founded on her disappointment with herself, always the little voice in her mind would scream "but you are *special.*"

Lula's mother fell ill and, virtually magically, Lula departed from her years of inner paradox. Somehow losing her mom wasn't special at all. At her age, several of her friends had suffered significant losses. Lula continued to feel not-special in the waiting room adjacent to the radiation treatments where family members flipped magazine pages as they waited to paste fake smiles on themselves when the techs brought them their dying relatives, all involved exhausted from the hurry-up-and-wait demands of a last illness.

Lula also didn't feel special at the cemetery when her mother was placed under six feet of Texas dirt even though her mother was possibly the best dressed person in attendance, wearing her best pink designer suit and encased in a $5,000 coffin.

Lula's housework clothes weren't unique either as she scrubbed the sickroom where her mother actually crossed over into some great beyond that was supposed to be special. Lula received no glimpse of that, her own eyes blinded like every other living person.

She began to sort out her mother's belongings so that relatives could select. She left until last the plastic bin with all the non-iPhone pictures thrown in. Lula did not cry a single tear, non-special that she was.

She let the record of her typical childhood filter onto the floor, occasionally setting aside a picture one of the relatives might want. At the very bottom of the bin, in a yellowing linen envelope, a brown edged photograph appeared as if by magic: a diapered, but otherwise naked, toddler with wild brown curls held out her balancing arms, fingers splayed. A look of triumph brazened on her own face through the fading gray of the picture. Lula herself, surrounded by Sunday-dressed relatives – her grandparents, aunt and uncle, her parents – in her grandmother's back yard. Everyone was clapping, their bodies leaning forward, their hands ready to catch her should she fall, all of them smiling, glorying in Lula's success.

Lula fell cross-legged to the floor, her special hands clutching the picture with wet fingers.

The Way of the World

MY SKIN WOULD tingle if the boy I loved in college was anywhere close. I searched for him as I walked to my classes in between red brick buildings with white wooden windows. I kept my head bowed, my eyes averted so that my tendency toward stalking wouldn't be noticed. Always I left my dorm coiffed and made up, a prize always on the market.

Now the love I have is voyeuristic and without cost. It is easier to hide now since I live by phone or iPad or YouTube videos of the few who experience the world outside, making choices, taking actions. Maybe celebrity talented, but probably just lucky.

They're photographed in the open air where skin can prickle from proximity and glances might meet between classes.

II.

LISTEN

PEOPLE ALL AROUND TELL THEMSELVES THEIR OWN STORY

My Brother's Keeper at the Funhouse

AT THE FUNHOUSE, a loudspeaker blared nonsensical sentences interrupted randomly by specific directions: Gibberish! Gibberish! Gibberish! TURN LEFT!!! Gibberish!

If a person wasn't paying close attention, they would miss the directives being blared and bump into moving walls. My dad helped me focus; he held my hand tightly in his larger one and pulled me gently in the direction I was supposed to take until finally we stood on a rocking floor, between two mirrors. The mirrors faced each other but were slightly ajar so that by looking forward, we were fat, and looking behind, we were rail thin. The mirrors were not as tall as Dad so neither of us threw up, but the girl next to me did and her mom did too.

As her sour smell exploded, Dad yanked me closer to him so that I wouldn't get her mess on my shoes. Something must've happened though because that sickening vomit-smell was with us even in the car as we drove home. "So, what did you think about the funhouse," he said.

"Gross. And creepy too. With nothing stable or anything."

"Odd word to use, son: creepy."

"You know that icky feeling you get if the teacher is accusing the class in general and then you know who did whatever it was she was talking about? Or creepy like Janice Ledder telling lies about the monsters in her room...totally ridiculous actually but yucky all the same."

"That's imagination for you, son," Dad answered.

I pinched my nose to fight the vomit smell. "That little kid next to me was really gross."

"She certainly did…we'll clean you up as soon as we get home You might have to take a bath."

"Did you ever get vomit all over you when you were a kid like me? Maybe even get to stay home because of it?"

His father laughed a bit. "Your grandmother made sure I went to school no matter what." He turned down our street. "I had the chicken pox once though. Had to stay in bed with that."

"Gross," I said and imagined his big frame in the bed at Grandma's, with polka-dotted feet hanging over the edge. "Were you all alone at home when Grandma went to work?" Grandma was chief buyer at a local women's clothing store and had been so for as long as I could remember. It had a candy section in the basement.

"I was only a kid. Maybe seven or eight. Way too young to be alone in the house."

"What did you do all day? What did you even think about?" The thought of nothing to do was new. "How did you do without recess? I hate Janice Ledder but at least someone's talking during recess. But boy, she talks a lot."

"Daydreams mostly I imagine," Dad said.

"About what? Superman? Monsters?"

He laughed again. "Who even remembers their childhood," he said but he seemed to be talking to himself, not to me. "Mostly a person just forgets things like that." He tapped my knee. "And that's probably best. You'd like to forget a few things, right? Getting in trouble stealing that candy at Grandma's store, huh?"

I felt a little queasy every time that came up; I'd like to just ignore that whole experience. "I bet Janice Leddar never ever forgets that she talks about that monster every single recess. Cause it's the spittin' image of her father she says. And she repeats that story till everyone is sick of it. Nobody will even play with her anymore. She repeats it over and over, like she's studying for a spelling test. Nobody ever listens anymore, not even the teacher. Maybe she should go to the funhouse so she can talk about something else."

We turned into our drive. "But Janice Leddar is really short and she'd probably throw up like that kid. Get vomit all over her like me."

Lula's Strategy for Keeping Secrets from Her Grown Daughter, Who Always Overreacts

WHEN YOUR HUSBAND dies, just omit that you have to self-pleasure to keep calm.

Don't discuss that you can't bear to go to the cemetery or that it makes you furious every time you drive by it.

If she doesn't realize you've had Botox and your lips plumped, why should *you* admit it? You just want to look rested. It's not like you got a facelift or anything. For that, you'd have to *directly* lie about where you've been. Although she probably wouldn't notice a thing even if you got one.

Whatever you do, refuse to admit you gave up white cotton panties for black lace thongs. After all, one never knows what'll happen.

Keep taking that estrogen; it's years 'til she'll see the Medicare bills. Who cares if the government doesn't pay for it? They should: it's their moral duty.

Under no circumstances mention that your girlfriends are getting you dates or that you go to bars with men you've just met at church. Children just don't understand how lonely a person can get.

If your estate lawyer just *insists*, you can show her your new will and all the financial statements. Financial statements don't have to list what you've bought. If Frank knows from heaven, well, he can just be mad. Some day, God forbid, your daughter will probably understand just how tempting it is to numb yourself at Neiman Marcus. You spending her inheritance is *your own business!*

Never talk about crying or being maudlin or desperate. Do not tell her about the pictures you couldn't stand to see every day and stuffed in the guest room closet. And absolutely do not mention the stockpile of Tylenol P.M. you've hidden in the bottom drawer of the night table. After all, these feelings might pass and there's no reason to get her all frantic and have to fight her on the nursing home thing.

There's absolutely no reason to clarify how you met her father in the first place. She'd never accept you were alone in a strip club by mistake. The whole myth you and Frank made up is just fine and it actually *could've* happened that Granny Belle introduced you to each other. There are just things she does not need to know. The only thing that should matter to her is that you and Frank loved each other, made a baby, and gave her a good life.

The dizzy spells in the shower are nobody's affair. You *can* take care of yourself and besides, you had a handrail installed on your *own* initiative. Dizzy spells mean nothing; the doctor said so.

If you forget your beauty parlor appointment, just let it go. The only person who should care is Flora, the stylist who replaced Holly who replaced Suzette who replaced whoever it was twenty years ago.

If you neglect to pack those thongs when you're on your way to visit her in California, don't fret. Just buy some new ones once you get there. Or else wash one out with the jumbo-size Ivory that, for some reason, you stuck in your bag.

Puffy eyes should be no one's concern. A person can always claim allergies and deny not being able to sleep. Everybody worries. You don't want to plant death and dementia and not-enough-money in her mind.

If a person can't remember someone's name right after being introduced at church, it is just not that big a deal. For one thing, it's your daughter's church and all those hippy-people talk after the worship. It is way too loud in there for God, not to mention yourself. Maybe that woman didn't even *say* her name. Now if you'd forgotten your daughter's name, that'd be an entirely different story.

There is absolutely *no reason* to mention the incident with the rental car. It was the agent's fault anyway; he should never have insisted on that hybrid, which makes no sound whatsoever so a person has no idea it's still turned on when they get out. Plus why would they even *make* a car that didn't require a key in the ignition.? Locking the keys in the car is just way too easy, causing no end of trouble for all concerned.

No matter how funny it is to you, just *shut your mouth* when you start to admit the security line at the airport. That TSA woman doesn't know anyone you know, and therefore cannot tell anyone you insisted your bag hadn't come through the scanner thing-y while you were leaning against it the whole time.

Going on and on about how real life is all encapsulated in each moment will bore your daughter to death, and even on that FaceTime thing she'll be rolling her eyes which you hate. The toddler-grandsons get it and that really should be enough for you.

Revealing your excursions with Theo on the back of his Harley would just be unkind of you. Listening to your daughter harangue about safety helmets will not change the fact that under no circumstances are you going to smash your hair down. Plus no one should be required to hear about rear-views of their muffin top or their more-than-ample buttocks. Theo faces forward, keeps his eyes on the road and tucks his gray locks behind his ears. He doesn't see a thing.

Serious Concerns

or

Weather.com Predicts Austin Tornado as Halloween Approaches

OVERHEAD THE SKY is threatening but to be ignored: weather won't be here until late tonight, so says Weather.com. Consequently my best friend Paula pulls up in her Range Rover outside the Austin Hilton to pick me up and we drive to her favorite restaurant to catch up, share details of our current experience, and trade the serious concerns we hold dear.

Parking near the restaurant costs $15 but we pay because it's convenient for us. We take a picture of our parking spot with the phone; the new iPhone camera misses no detail even in this darkening light.

Our heels click on the uneven pavement as we walk to the restaurant. We tuck our shoulder bags tightly under our arms because ahead we notice a suspicious couple who seem quite different from us. At first they appear to be window-shopping or looking inside for someone they know, but as we get closer, we see his hands on his hips, humping in mock intimacy. As we approach, we notice they each have dreadlocks tied behind their ears into ponytails and their clothes are shabby, once colorful but now faded and worn. We catch a whiff of their rancid odor as we draw near. The air is heavy with the coming rain but evidently the storm is theoretical to everyone although Paula and I have been in storms before. We don't know about these two.

The couple turns from the window as if they sense us. He says, "Some change toward a sandwich?" She says, "Soooooo hungry." Neither of us makes eye contact with them. They are an idea to us, an idea not on the news or in the papers, on Facebook or the Internet.

We think: looks like drugs to us. Drugs is something each of us knows more about than we would like to know and we're terrified of providing overdoses. "Not today," we answer in unplanned unison. We do not speak of what we saw.

We push the heavy glass door of the restaurant inward but ignore our reflections in the glass, do not recognize the distortions of it. We give our names to the hostess. She leads us to our candlelit table where we order wine and salads. These are delivered quickly and we both ask for the veal piccata entrée although we neglect to discuss the cruelty of producing veal. Instead we enjoy the white, well-seasoned delicacy as we share the details of our existence and our serious concerns while the tornado-laden weather moves into Austin. That storm, like each and every storm, will drench many and drown a few.

You Can't Sit Still While You're Trying to Swim
No Matter What They Tell You

FIRST, THEY TAKE away swimming ... warm, safe, with no effort necessary for breathing. You get squeezed out as some voice screams, "Wait, hold back just a second," and then, "Now push!" Lights assault you, penetrate even eyes tight shut. A few days later, They slice your penis while someone holds you still somewhere you don't smell your mother, only pee. You need to wiggle wiggle wiggle.

You may think you've lost everything, but then They take away sucking and a full warm tummy and your smiling mommy looking into your eyes. You wiggle some more.

They bring in some other kid to replace you and They force you to say it's cute. You stomp your foot and demand They take that intruder back to the big cold building that smells like pee.

The plastic bucket thing is right next to you all the time and the rule is you have to pee *here*. Everything seems to be about pee or being nice to your brother. Not about a full tummy or sitting in your mommy's lap while she reads you *Goodnight Moon*.

You get squeezed into clothes and forced to Sit Still in church and at dinner, and during nap time, you have to Be Still. It's the same at school; They tell you school is the most wonderful place in the world, which it is not. When you are there They take away your slingshot and make you tie your sneakers all the time. They won't let you chase the children in skirts or call them names, even though those kids have cooties. They also won't let you play war. Over and over again you have to Sit Still.

This goes on forever—all the way to college except They eventually let you chase girls instead of boys—only then at parties where beer is mostly free. If you happen to be unable to Sit Still, They let you play war but then it's not as fun because They might cut off your leg or your arms. Even if They don't slash you, though, They will certainly take away your sleep by interrupting it with nightmares and panic attacks about foreign wars.

If you don't play war, and also even if you do, then They end up taking all your recess and force you to study all the time to make up for not Sitting Still.

If you chase a lot of girls, They eventually force you into abandoning all except one. You may even think that's fine until She turns into Them and takes away your fun by turning off the sports channel and stealing—with malice and forethought—your peace and quiet by dumping babies in your lap and going shopping. Needless to say, They wipe out your money. Plus She insists you Sit Still and listen to harangues until you finally are able to smooth things over with sex, which is quickly over but occasionally satisfactory.

Little by little They screw the bolts tight and force you to Sit Still every minute of every day in another one of those big buildings that smells like pee. Time passes and you might think things are generally OKAY until people you care about start dropping as slowly as your pee does into the toilet these days. Rob your Army buddy starts dressing like the girls he used to chase and Fred's heart explodes so fast medics don't reach him. Then David Jakes admits he fantasizes about you more than his girlfriend of ten years and would you like to run away with him? Pretty much,

They've taken over your reality and distorted it like the kaleidoscope you once found in your Christmas stocking.

One day you shed your clothes in front of the wife's full-length mirror and see nothing but wrinkles and folds on your knees, your butt. Even your feet don't look like your feet when you bend down over the gut that is now a bit less rounded out from not drinking anymore and replacing booze with increasing nicotine. You lean your face forward and discover They've taken the brown from your hair and your beard, even your nose hair and the little tufts on your chest. Brown is replaced with silvery stuff but not the monetary kind.

Finally They—or someone They ignore—starts taking away your breath. You start huffing and puffing while climbing the stairs. The one thing you *ask* Them to take away, the tumor in your lung, They insist on you keeping and They force you to Sit Still while They shine another highly unsatisfactory beam on your body that ends up burning your skin like hell. They stick a little tube in your nose. The tube eliminates running and eventually walking, let alone chasing girls or playing war or shooting spit wads with your slingshot.

You begin to see that pretty soon They're going to take away the thing inside that's really you. They stole—repeat: *stole!*—your belief that stuff happens to other people and not to you. Plus, even stole your hope for an escape that somehow still hides in the back of your mind.

They stick you in a room of the building that still smells like pee. On a Tuesday, in the corner you see Rob or Frank or David, all of whom already crossed the divide you now recognize but They keep denying. Your friends don't seem to be doing anything; they're just standing there waiting for you to stop breathing. The room that smells like pee, and everything in it, feels like just one big demand They set up, like a principal would in a schoolroom where no one gets to do what they want.

They insist it's time you hand over your breath, but as has always been the case, They want to take it away before you're ready. You want to beat the odds like Lazarus. You wonder if that's Jesus standing at the end of your bed with everyone ignoring Him. You've no real trouble with Him—it's all the other authorities that enrage you—all of Them—even though, you are now definitely Being Still.

Someone offers you a crystal goblet in which fizzy champagne glistens like sun bouncing off water. You can't seem to hold the glass—so They take it away and pour a tiny bit into a plastic medicine cup. It sloshes like a tornado in the center of a swimming pool. You sip champagne. It tickles your nose. You smile without even trying but They take it away from you all the same.

Forms of Defiance 2:
Promises Made to Self
Abandoned Due to Inadequacy

The Expectation: At least tell *God* the truth.

An Insult: The *real* truth.

Wrinkles

CHAOS DOESN'T GET better...and in the mind, it makes crazy, eating up all my time, telling me lies and stealing innocence even in the presence of innocence.

My mother's mental illness probably started with her own chaos, and then she perpetuated mine. Though the actual memory of her phobic behavior eludes me, I deduce such because of my automatic terror at disorder.

For example, if faced with a calculus test here at college I become obsessed with tidying my dorm room, then wiping every cleared surface with Lysol or whatever bleach I can afford. Next, I "must" tidy my calendar, scheduling healthy meals from the dorm cafeteria, and hope I can get there early enough to avoid the spoiled eggs and leftover grease from Amy Jones setting her bacon beside her tray. Finally, I "must" update my list of duties: near term, next week, and long term, scheduling my life in advance.

Please note the immediate list includes stealing, then disposing of, Jane's pet lizard held in a small wine case on her side of the dorm room. Three doors down but still, quite an awful pet to have: disgusting.

On the intermediate list, I need to figure out the best way to break up with Tom Adams since I saw the sun god tattoo he has on his side – low, near his ass. I saw it when we were fucking night before last. Tom Adams can never fill the slot of husband on the long-term list. Worshiping a sun god with a tattoo will not, under any circumstances, make order out of chaos, as my dad made order for my mother.

Not to mention that although Tom Adams is the top pre-med student at this university, he followed through with fucking though I told him not to. It isn't orderly for a girl to take such a chance on unmarried pregnancy.

It isn't really a loss of innocence that's important – after all isn't chaos itself such a loss and an extreme one at that?

The consequences of pregnancy can mean chaos-on-steroids because Tom Adams wouldn't marry me if his life depended on it. That's because I reminded him that a sun god tattoo especially in such a spot on a body as his would eventually wrinkle and sag, forcing everyone who saw it into a godless form of disgust.

Oral Fixation:
The Path of My Personal Life

DEAD TO THE world, I finally fight the newborn sun streaming through the window onto the bed. I disentangle myself from my husband, suck down the necessary sixteen ounces of caffeine (heavy on the milk). I exchange my pink silk night-skin for something more serious, head for my home office. I had dreamed of my mother who in real life morphed from mother-in-control-of-the-universe to childlike dependence within a year. I needed to think that dream through.

I reach for my new copy of *Necessary Losses*. Judith Viorst, the author, told me lots of people are trying to get back to their mother's womb where there aren't any boundaries between them and their host; they are essentially the same person.

Then I happened on a review of this new book of Hemingway's letters. The reviewer seems to think Hemingway expressed this repeated desire to live a boundary-less life, which I deduce relates to his life in utero. Or perhaps he just didn't like paying his bills. Running across this review was really a surprising coincidence, especially today, just months since my own mother died her difficult death and the recurring dreams. The mysteriousness of seeing this review today is a connection that may underlie my reaction to Hemingway, or maybe not.

Necessary Losses tells me a person can experience this kind of oneness in orgasm, art, or drugs, all of which I presume Hemingway must have experienced as a matter of course. *Necessary Losses* says we can recreate the oneness with fantasies, or even dreams too, I suppose, which perhaps explains the art part of Hemingway's life. And maybe the orgasm part too for all I know. The drug aspect seems a bit more difficult to prove because after all who really saw him enough of the time? Of course, he was evidently a big drinker of alcohol, which is a lot like drugs or so I hear.

But what this scenario doesn't explain is why Hemingway hated his mother in the first place, which is widely claimed but who can really say? Mothers are, after all, vital when it comes to oneness and being fed and mostly being cared for at all. Fathers are supposed to be at work.

Necessary Losses and also this review don't really explain why aficionados of Hemingway, like my husband, are obsessed with hunting and fishing and bullfighting. Or even why the wives of such aficionado-husbands are obsessed with Prada handbags from Neiman Marcus except Prada purses and shotguns could be construed to be substitutes for thumb-sucking. Or even substitutes for love itself.

But maybe Prada purses and shotguns are merely expressions of an over-supply of hormones essential to orgasm. Unless of course a deficit exists, in which case depression ensues and bankruptcy results, which in turn negates the Prada purses, shotguns, memberships at the Dallas Country Club and most Texas hunting leases.

These are things I don't believe Hemingway experienced but perhaps I am wrong. He may have gone hunting in West Texas, but it would've been quail or perhaps bucks he shot instead of safari animals—which I suppose would be a *Necessary Loss* for the animals anyway and maybe a thumb-sucking activity for Hemingway.

Of course, we mustn't forget Hemingway killed himself with a shotgun and very often that is done by first placing the steel barrel in one's mouth much like a thumb or a binky. The reality was Hemingway shot himself in the forehead, but for such a man as he, I suppose brain and mouth are about the same thing, both being communication devices. I would imagine the result is a very messy process most mothers would not like at all, maybe even with screams and tears. After all, that blood and everything is a lot like expelling a fetus and cutting the cord.

An Antidote for Writer's Block
or
Retreat Retreat Retreat

"…alone with all that could happen…"
from a story by William H. Gass

Alone with all that can happen
… but does not.
a blank page by CCS

Eggs

THE KITCHEN HAD that odor, sulfurous and dank. Suzette had forgotten to run the disposal last night when she cleaned up dinner. There would be hell to pay if Brett realized she hadn't cleaned it up properly.

Quickly, before Brett woke up, she rummaged in the fridge, found some leftover watermelon chunks and ground them up in her $3,000 sink, product of Brett's settlement at the hospital. He hadn't been able to get along with anyone there.

The smell was moderated, but she still noticed it and knew Brett would too. He'd be insinuating all day.

This difficulty distracted her a bit, but only a bit, from the ringing in her ear, which had started weeks ago but to which no one could give a name. Her internist could find nothing amiss and even Brett, who always had an answer for everything, was flummoxed, though he had scoured the internet and finally was searching the hospital library. He had found nothing but of course was still looking. "Your health is everything, Suzette. What would I do if something happened to you?"

Being married to a mind like Brett had its advantages but it hadn't worked this time. This morning she wanted him to stay asleep while this smell dissipated and she figured out how to deflect the inevitable interrogation about the ringing.

Years ago, she had become a decent liar to make things easier with Brett. No matter what the subject, be it something in their daily life or a book they'd read or an event on the news, he just always out-thought her. Their discussions could, in an instant,

73

disintegrate into his clear disdain for her feeble attempts at expressing any point at all. She would fall into apologies he wouldn't accept, not really, and feel like the world's most pathetic partner.

When they'd met in college, they had been equals of a sort if enrolled in different doctoral programs, Brett in microbiology and she in English. He understood the natural world and she the literary one. She had had so many friends, but he was a loner, frustrated with the limitations of his colleagues. She came to understand that, on some level, probably an unconscious one, he believed his work was more important than hers. "Without the body," he would say, "surely nothing else matters."

After medical school, his mantra was "I hold others' life in my hands, my mind," while she just taught stories to undergraduates. She couldn't seem to convince him that the stories might alter the entire course of a person's life, or else explain the meaning of life to those patients of his. In her deepest self, though, she knew her understanding to be true.

Sometimes she *did* feel a fraud compared to him, as if she misrepresented her own intellect even to herself. How could she not defend what she believed even about so small a thing as leftover deviled eggs or how to clean up after dinner?

Who was she really? Wasn't she just someone who had overreached? Or had she? It was after all she who practiced daily prayers, she who had searched out the soul-work of her life from all the resources she knew.

She wiped the counter with Lysol, poured some down the disposal, hoped for the best. She shook her head against the ringing in her ear. When Brett walked from their bedroom, she would serve him strong coffee, and say: "Rachel next door mentioned an article in the *Wall Street Journal* about ringing in the ears. I didn't actually see it, – for all I know, she made it all up – but maybe you should check it out." That would send him out the door for the morning. The smell would be gone by then and she would have the entire time for the novel she was reading.

She reminded herself: 'I do *love* Brett,' but in spite of that genius of his, not because of it. She admitted to herself once again that it was a plague to him and to everybody else. He was an Icarus who didn't see he had made wings of wax, not of flesh. He would keep flying up and up in hubris obsession too close to a real sun that would melt the wax little by little. In his myth, he would fall in silence and in silence, all alone.

Two for One: Units of Meaning
or
Lula Tries to Make Sense of Her Life While Reading about Shakespearean Scenic Design on Page 28 of Book with Mostly the Same Name by Mark Rose

LULA BEGINS TO study the Bible in a closed-system manner at her Presbyterian Church, part of a denomination that, as the reader may know, is historically steeped in predestination. Predestination is an outgrowth of the Reformation of 1517, an outgrowth Lula imagines was propelled by the liberal wing of whatever political parties were available at the time. This confuses Lula quite a bit because the Bible seems to be crammed with many kinds of narratives but predestination seems more formula-like: the elect are saved but the non-elect are damned. Lula can't seem to put herself squarely in either category.

The Bible teacher suggests Lula do additional research to reassure herself, so Lula stacks up various explanations of strict cause-and-effect, such as *The Naked Now* by Richard Rohr, who seems to dismiss cause and effect as an inadequate interpretation of Christianity. Yet commentaries from John Calvin, the father of Calvinism and evidently the most intelligent man of his age, are dizzying in his conviction that God actually separates himself forever from some people. Richard Rohr seems slightly liberal, but John Calvin's ideas seem as airtight as a coffin. Lula can't figure out where she will land: heaven or hell.

Lula is called upon to teach the fourth graders at said Presbyterian Church because no one else will come forward to do it since those kids are so rambunctious. Sunday after Sunday, Preacher announces that no one has realized their calling. Lula can't stop feeling awkward and guilty because she doesn't have a regular job after all and she has spent all that time studying said Bible stories.

One week a child confesses that her parents fight and yell, one parent even throwing things across the room. Lula immediately contacts Preacher who replies, "We can't do a thing about it; it's theirs to work out." Preacher seems to believe so firmly in God's sovereignty that nobody's actions can change anything. His conclusion takes everyone off the proverbial hook but Lula can't help but wiggle a bit on that hook.

Later, long after Lula finishes the school year and successfully avoids church services before subsequent school years begin, Lula hears that this particular child may have lied in the past. Lula decides to believe this rumor because the child claimed not to have taken her Ritalin one Sunday morning though this child's mother was quite a responsible person.

Lula, in order to hold in her mind a tidy reality of Good versus Evil, along with the untidy (if organic) reality of parents ultimately being in authority over their daughters, begins to obsess over literary novels such as *East of Eden* by John Steinbeck. These books, though enclosed in covers (which means even novels are closed-ended in that way), at least nod in the direction of things not being completely explained by sacred texts or historical documents. Novels seem slightly open-ended, therefore open to interpretation. For example, in *East of Eden*, maybe that creepy madam at the end was abused as a child instead of being just a sociopath. But didn't she have a choice somewhere along the way? Lula finds all that ambiguity exhausting as well as frustrating and actually just as complicated as predestination. The whole issue just isn't all that easy to live with.

Lula keeps going back to the old Bible stories for inspiration because—in a never-ending circular pattern of struggle between her conscious mind and the irritating, nagging, not to mention *vague* discomfort of the recurring thought: 'Surely this cannot be all there is to it'—Lula can't seem to help herself.

Lula searches and searches but no conclusion shows itself. Finally she winds up here in *Shakespearean Design*, a good book but a fair amount over her head. She sees a chart that explains how intervening (seemingly unrelated) episodes set between major scenes can somehow act as thematic torpedoes. A short interchange between jesters might be set in between two highly emotional set pieces but point to the basic idea of the story, only in a different way, a funny way, forcing the reader to feel even more keenly whatever point Shakespeare was trying to make. This makes sense to Lula, but she still cannot figure out succeeding paragraphs; the Rose book does not explain how something on a page can be true while what it represents is false and incomplete. Lula is left wondering: Is she saved? Has she done what she needs to do to *be* saved or is there anything to be done? Or is she just crazy? Or finite (which could be another word for stupid) in the midst of an infinity that everyone seems to understand except her?

If she closes the books piled up on her bed and replaces them on the stack, perhaps she can just forget her eternal status entirely, along with the fact that she evidently will never understand the issue in the first place. After all it's an issue that mostly stays within the covers of said books. Lula can thus return to Reality TV and distract herself from agonizing over the fact that little girl in her class grew up without a teacher, the Church, or the Reformed Tradition.

Because She Was Rich

EVEN WHEN LAWRENCE died, she didn't have to work. She indulged herself by doing exactly what she wanted to do: read without interruption. She hired Jacinta to cook, and clean up, and run her errands. When she wanted something and couldn't find it online, she did have to go to the Used Bookseller and search. But this she didn't mind doing because she loved the musty, reliable smell of the unpainted, over-full shelves.

Books collected in heaps in the sitting room off her bedroom: novels she'd put off, histories that caught her fancy, and self-help guides that were analyzed in magazine articles. She forced herself to read the *Dallas Morning News* on Sunday mornings because she wanted to keep up with the outside world. Toward the end, though, she stopped reading everything except the reviews because it seemed to her that no one was thinking at all or applying what they should already know: that murderers needed psychiatrists instead of barbed wire, and children shouldn't be sent to war but to college, and if everyone stopped driving those odd tank-like cars, the Middle East oil sheiks could be left to their own devices.

When her breath became labored sometimes, Jacinta would ask if she could please please please dust the sitting room. "Absolutely not," she replied. "Just go around things as best you can. It's not that bad and . . . wheeze wheeze . . . if you really clean in there, you'll get my things out of order." Her real reason was because she loved the smell of her stacks: the crackling fresh paper scent of the new ones, and the whiff of ancient-ness of the old ones. Her neighbor, who tried to visit once a month, said: "You have *got* to go to a doctor."

The doctor prescribed asthma inhalers that kept getting themselves lost. On a Saturday night, she was in the middle of an article, "The Life of Flannery O'Connor," the part when Flannery was in the hospital for the last time and stuffing her manuscripts under her pillow so she could, against doctor's orders, continue to work on her stories. Flannery's decision to keep on in spite of everything was her gift to the rest of us, she thought, and promptly began the biography all over again. This time she read the stories Flannery wrote along the way, so as to be fully engaged with them as the author was during her outward life.

She drank hot tea made in the upstairs coffee bar, and ate from the extra-large package of Hostess cupcakes and the bags of vinegar-and-salt chips she'd stashed. She started to wheeze, reached for the inhaler, tapped her fingers around the floor to find it. The tightness in her chest got worse. "Stop dammit," she said to herself, and kept on with the sentence she was in the middle of.

"Jacinta," she called out, then realized it was now Sunday morning, Jacinta's day off. She put the book down, found the inhaler under the ottoman. She put her mouth to it, and tried to breathe in. Nothing much came out, but enough, she decided, and tossed it aside.

She thought to find a replacement, but remembered she hadn't ordered one yet. Her breath eased a bit. She fell back into Flannery O'Connor's life. Flannery was stuffing the draft of 'Parker's Back' under the pillow; nurse's shoes were clicking down that hall.

She too grabbed up 'Parker's Back.' So delicious a story she couldn't put it aside, she ignored the tightening of her nasal passages, her chest, and then the easing, then the tightening. She'd have to call the pharmacy . . . just as soon as Parker presented his Byzantine tattoo to his hateful wife. The pharmacy would bring another inhaler right to her; she was rich enough. Her wheeze was louder, and interfering with the story. Parker displayed the picture of Jesus on his back, was beaten by the hateful wife with a broom. How amazing to express that kind of rage. She wondered what that wife could possibly have lost to isolate herself with all that anger.

She coughed and the book fell from her hand; then she gasped. "Relax," she said to herself, grabbed up the book of stories again. Breathing seemed to race with Parker's developing act of grace: her breath in one lane and Parker's final despair in the other, racing toward the finish line.

A shaft of sunlight through her bedroom window demanded her attention, and it seemed as if she saw Parker rise and run through it, toward a figure waving two crutches, but not leaning upon them anymore. It came to her that it didn't matter one whit whether she was rich, or that she could read as long as she wanted, or that the inhaler could be delivered to her pronto if she would only call. She rose and chased Parker, leaving behind the cushy house with the cave-like sitting room, and the books tumbling to the floor.

The Cream Always Rises to the Top
or
The Hubris of the Envious Onlooker

GOD LOOKED DOWN (or over or up or through, depending on your point of view) at Baby Faulkner then turned Her (or His or It, again depending upon your perspective or ideas or theology) and took in Baby Hemingway.

She giggled.

She was in the mood for a little joke. She pointed her long, left finger at the world of Baby Hemingway and her right finger at the world of Baby Faulkner. She smiled at their sentences and pursed her lips at the worth of those words, but that's another story.

Then Satan showed up: that bad, bad penny. Satan tried to one-up God with a sin to afflict those babies with, but Satan has *no* creativity at all: he lost hold of it while he was falling, although he refused to accept the fact. Satan could come up with no sins at all. However, God thought it actually was a nice idea to give those boys-to-come a challenge to leap over. They needed something to write about anyway because writers is what She made them. No one knows plot points like God does.

She reached back into History and planted a few seeds that could come up while the boys lived, including decent whiskey and the limits of Time. Whiskey was pretty easy to insert in their lives but the limits of Time was a lot more interesting, being both practical and theoretical to Her way of thinking.

She was letting the idea of Time percolate through History and then through Albert Einstein's life...just to keep things really going.

She leaned back in her comfy chair and let Life unfold while Alice Munro took a seat next to Anton Chekhov. The three were all real close, although unconscious, friends. God found Alice relaxing and enjoyed watching her play with things. Alice found God ... well, you know.

Point. Click.

Start with the subject. A subject doesn't have to be totally fleshed out at first—you don't have to know *everything* about them – what's in their drawers and all, unless the junk drawer or something is what you're photographing. Then search search search to find that character's face somewhere, anywhere.

While you're looking, be scrupulous in caring for your kids—don't avoid them or forget they've got to eat and sleep and get to school on time. If you make a mistake with them, you'll hear about it from the authorities in your life and there'll be hell to pay.

Pretty much nobody will ever accept the excuse that you were looking for a particular person to take a picture of. Pretty much everyone thinks the camera is just a hobby – a pastime you can control if you really want, if you love your kids. It's better not to correct other adults – they'll just think you're crazy and it'll stir up self-doubt as well.

Remember that eventually children grow up, and husbands either leave or die. By that time, it's entirely possible you'll have found the subject's face, taken the picture, and sold it to *Aperture Magazine* or someplace that'll make you equally famous. You'll be able to relax, having done what you were created to do in the first place. People will understand then and, in their memories, make allowances.

They leave. All of them—both children, and the thoroughly discontented husband. The husband made lots of money, enough to go around. You cry your tears, comfort your children, but underneath the grief pulses a long-lost relief. You clean the house top to bottom, rid yourself of the extraneous miscellany that distracted you from the camera. You excise the unnecessary from your closets, your cupboards, the garage, even your Rolodex. Just wad up the business card of your neighbor two doors down who went professional doing landscapes; cram it into the trash bag. Take a deep breath, make every effort to dispel your wish that her son gets into drugs.

Your fingers caress the camera at the top of the closet where it's mostly been during the time it's taken for your family to get their own lives. Some years you only took it off the shelf if it fit into your suitcase on family vacations. Or when someone asked you to take pictures of their kids for free. You took a few courses, entered a few contests, even earned a little money. Not enough, however, to justify friends or babysitters or nannies to drive your kids to the opportunities you knew they'd resent not having when they grew up.

But now they *are* grown-up. One is in Europe studying economics so she can make her daddy proud. The other's a history major at the state university. They don't come home much. The history major called to tell you she's taking another art class, this time a photography class, next semester. You're confused by your queasiness when she told you. You want her to appreciate art, even made her take lessons once. During the semester, she asked for extra money in her allowance so she could buy more film. You got queasy again, swallowed to keep what shouldn't come to consciousness from coming to consciousness. "Of course, honey," you answered, and sent the money.

You force yourself to go out and snap pictures. This time you go to the local Starbucks with the other mommies retired from duty. As you point, click, and smile to gain cooperation, you secret the knowledge that you aren't like them at all. You think you recognize the character you've always searched for – blue eyes overly made-up and black hair streaked with gray – and you feel a momentary relief. It turns out to be nothing—the woman has a red scar across the side of her face you didn't see at first—and you know that the very visibility of it ruins the character's mystery. For some other artist, of course, the scar would be the mystery, but not for you.

Your daughter comes home for spring break. Proudly, she opens a black leather portfolio her boyfriend gave her for Christmas. She pulls out ten black and white 11 x 14's on resin-coated paper. They are landscapes and strangers' faces and the implements of people's jobs—a tree studded median on a highway, a white tramp with a sparkly coat, and rusting shovels against a garage door. They are good photographs, really good. With a pinch of vanity, you imagine them hanging on a museum wall. The printing, she reports, was called "exquisite" by her teacher, who happens to be famous, and you must agree.

Your daughter speaks. "I love it *so* much. My teacher says I can change majors and only lose a semester and a half. Do you think Dad will pay? Do you? If not, I don't care. I've got to do this. I just can't believe I'm only now realizing what I want to do with my life."

Your daughter's face is alight. She's never looked more herself. Your heart softens, glad for her, but you run to the bathroom and lean over the toilet anyway. The bile is the worst thing you've ever tasted—acidic, bitter. Worse, even, than the morning sickness you had for nine months—with both girls—while other women suffered only three.

You fear you'll never rid yourself of the taste. You splash cold water on your cheeks, in your mouth. When you lift your hot face up, and run your tongue over your teeth, your eyes meet your eyes in the mirror. Notice the daylight from the window bounces off the sprinkle of silver in your hair. You long for your camera. A proper darkroom for after the picture is snapped.

"And you'll support me to Dad, won't you?" she calls from the other room.

Avert your eyes.

Avert eyes.

Avert.

Rule of Three
or
Various Ways Lula Sought to Numb Herself to the Discomfort of Her Responsibilities: Call Her Mother, Go to the Grocery and Attend the Opening of Stewart's Art Exhibit

Tap Tap Tap   Tap Tap Tap TapTapTapTap   One Ring-y Ding-y, Two Ring-y Ding-y, Three Ring-y Ding-y Click

Tap Tap Tap   Pork Chops for Company

Tap Tap Tap   Directions to Craighead Gallery

Tap Tap Tap   FlipBoard News ... Tap ... Celebrity

Tap Tap Tap   Kate & William Impress Huge Crowds in Australia

Tap Tap Tap   What Kate Wore ... Tap ... Alexander McQueen Sells Out in 8 Seconds!

Tap Tap Tap   Kate's Style Evolution

Tap Tap Tap   Amazon.Com ... Tap ... Great Dresses of the 20th Century

Tap Tap Tap	Great Outfits of the 20th Century
Tap Tap Tap	Adolf Hitler's Mustache and Its Impact on History
Tap Tap Tap	Sociopaths in the History of Man
Punch Twist Lift	Glug Glug Glug … gulp
Click Click Click	the Millionaire Matchmaker

Glug Glug Glug … glug glug glug … gulp

Click Click Click	The Bachelorette
Tap Tap Tap	Reality Steve's Spoilers / Bachelorette 7 / What Happened Tonight
Tap Tap Tap	Solitaire for Geniuses

Gulp Gulp Gulp ….. Gulp Gulp Gulp

Zzz zzz zzz zzz zz z

On Fragmenting Family Myth in the Interest of Maintaining Sanity Amidst Imperfection, Sin and Character Flaws

THE FATHER WAS the perfect soul: quiet, bookish, and of impeccable character, but who was also possessed of a ribald sex drive, or maybe it was just an over stimulated testosterone gland. But wait … perhaps he was just OCD about being honest because *his* father, the Grandfather, had PTSD from WWI and became a Freemason which as everyone knows (since it's a fact on the Internet) has really strict guidelines about moral behavior. Or maybe the Father just loved the Mother—maybe his sex drive was only directed at her … There are rumors about their vigorous pleasure at all times of the day, but of course those rumors originated with the Mother after the Father was safely buried.

The Father worked hard, that's a measurable fact, although he was not an educated man unless you count as education his purchase of *The Great Books of the Western World* (a 'Harvard education on a bookshelf'). All the Father's children fought over the set after the Father was safely buried. The Daughter ended up mailing them to the Brother at great expense some time after the Father's funeral.

The Father labored diligently, it is said, and everyone certainly observed him being absent from family life; he was eventually a traveling salesman. With lots of friends in that business, he became a 'rag man' after he almost went bankrupt after an entrepreneurial effort. The Father would leave the house on Mondays and be gone until Friday afternoons late, although somehow he always made it to any event in which one of his children appeared either as star in school performances or just participant.

He schlepped sample cases around all day while his own clothes hung in antiseptic motel rooms—along with a slowly escaping bottle of whiskey and his current book, its bookmark steadily marching toward the back cover day by day. It is a guess about the location of the booze ... he may have left that on the car's seat beside him in case he had an extra five minutes that didn't belong to anyone. It is also a guess about the current book; that may have been perched on the car seat too, as the Daughter does when she drives carpool. One can only fantasize what he did about that sex drive/attraction to the Mother/high testosterone level, though one somehow doubts he'd be into self-stimulation. But it is true he looked at his mail on Fridays before he greeted anyone or kissed the Mother hello so who knows.

The IRS evidently thought the Father was indeed the most honest person around ... or at least they only audited him once that anyone remembers. The agent was a woman named Heidi and she boasted the shoulders of a weight lifter or a defensive back and also coincidentally happened to be in the Daughter's graduate management class. If anyone could've fragmented the Father's honesty, it might have been Heidi, but since the Father never went to jail, maybe the fragmentation didn't even happen. Evidently, Heidi could find no fault line. No one is certain. The Daughter did hear her parents express a great deal of resentment toward the IRS for keeping the Father off the Rag Man Road where the money was made.

I'd bet all the family would like to have been an actual bug in the Father's brain all those years if only to know the exact dimensions of the myth. It would have been a relief to be completely in his head instead of their own. But now he's safely buried so being in his head wouldn't be all that illuminating. It's dark in there.

Eyeglasses

I WANT TO talk to my mother, but she is dead. I normally call her every morning to bitch about my life, my late marriage, the things only a mother will listen to.

She died five Saturdays ago after yet another bout of lung cancer. We thought Mom would pull through again as she had before. Instead she asked me if I "could do it," by which she meant could I accompany her to the edge while she died. Not my genius brother Tom or my entrancing sister Kerry – but me. I'm the oldest one but the least sure of most things, a stark contrast to my confident mother, who seemed to know exactly the trajectory on which she found herself. Compared to Tom or Kerry, I am a double-minded mess. Of course, in true family fashion, I answered: "I'll try." I noticed her eyeglasses were askew, but I did not adjust them.

She raised trembling fingers holding her wine glass to her lips. "Make sure Kerry gets Gran's china and Tom the family Bible. You don't need anything honey; you've had Jake. By Jake she meant my late husband who was the only financial success we are related to. She sipped, the wine slopping the sides of the glass, then added: "Bury me with the little angel in the pretty-things cabinet, the one with spade in her hands. Cause I've finished my row." By this she referred to her old adage of "keep on keeping on." Very melodramatic, like all of her declarative sentences, but also truer than true.

Mom drank that wine slowly and deliberately, as if it were her very last which it did turn out to be. She sighed, handed the wineglass to me, then stared into the corner of her bedroom, her forehead wrinkled and quizzical. Her papery fingers lifted to the stems of her eyeglasses, looked over the top, then set them back in place again. Her hand shook when she raised it and pointed toward the corner of the room, let it fall when words evidently failed her. "It's time for me to rest now," she said. Her eyeglasses dropped on the blanket; she ignored my outstretched hand.

I helped settle her awkward bulk, but she still appeared uncomfortable with her labored breathing, her weakened limbs. I didn't know what else to do.

Her eyeglasses were quite wonderful – a foray into opulence quite atypical of Mom, the lenses in an ivory-white encasement speckled with crystal insets. I put them back on her face, but she removed them and set them back into my hand, wordless, still staring into the corner.

How I wish I had asked her what she saw but I was stunned at the entire situation. How does one stand without a floor to stand on?

I want to call my mother and tell her about a dress I saw over at Neiman Marcus. Some way, I have to settle on a dress for this wedding I object to – my daughter, Suzette's. I pick up the phone to dial, realize that I can't talk to her anymore. Realize she is forever absent.

Besides advice on the dress, I need her help with the holidays. I feel a surge of resentment that Kerry took our grandmother's china although I'm the one who has to cook Thanksgiving dinner. The recipe for Red Apples isn't within the ancient rubber band of necessary holiday offerings. Perhaps I just missed it, and I retrieve the crystal-stemmed eyeglasses waiting for whatever they're waiting for on the kitchen counter, dial my sister.

I haven't seen Kerry since I cleaned out Mom's house and everyone came to pick through. I'd filched the glasses before anyone showed up. "Kerry," I said, "I need the Red Apple recipe."

"Are you out of your mind? I'm teaching a class and can't risk getting fired over Red Apples."

"Well, look as soon as you get home." I slammed the phone down. At least Mom wouldn't hear about that slam. I'd get chewed out over it, Mom would be judgmental and I'd feel guilty; Kerry would get off Scot-free.

I leave Mom's eyeglasses on, though things are fuzzy for me. I abandon Thanksgiving dinner prep, try to read, end up flipping through a stack of catalogues, think again about the Neiman's dress, feel myself tense over Suzette's damn boy. Would my mother even approve of that dress?

I wish I knew what Mom saw in the corner before she breathed her last. Was it Dad? Was it Gran or Pop? Or maybe someone else – like God or Jesus or one of her old boyfriends, someone else. My eyes start to water but I feel embarrassed, silly. People at sixty-five lose their parents.

My need to talk to Mom about Suzette marrying Donald is mired in desperation as I think about it. Mom would be able to devise a plan to avert this disaster – she always was so *sure* she could work things out – although I never would've admitted it. But Mom's buried and I still need someone who can advise me how to talk Suzette out of this; Donald is a mess and he's going to eventually be a financial mess. Mother has gone to her reward as the saying goes. What reward is there though when a person is so absolutely sure of their opinions? Did Mom get kudos or gold mansions or seventy-three virgins for always knowing exactly what should be done in every situation? Or did she get a shock by evaporating into molecules because that corner of hers held nothing.

I slip on the eyeglasses to distract myself with the bride's magazines Suzette demanded I peruse; fortunately, the pages are quite indistinct. Suzette stuck little notes on the pages of her ridiculous choices: a couture dress at $7,500, a barbecue wedding luncheon, and monogrammed hand towels for favors. Every choice seems off somehow, wrong at the deepest level. If I could tell Mom, she would just say that it's because I hate Donald. Suzette also insists on a calligrapher to address invitations to a zillion people; she wants me to quickly produce a list of every relative that lives in the USA. I don't even know most of those people and anyway, have no addresses.

As I always do, I struggle to keep my connection with Suzette by avoiding contradicting her adult choices, so I call Tom. The list of family members is in the first page of the family Bible, and I halfway remembered a list of addresses being there too. Of course, Tom doesn't answer his phone; he certainly never ignored Mom.

If only Mom were here, she would guide me through, tell me how to get rid of Donald without getting rid of Suzette. I wonder if Mom ever faced a problem like Donald, then I think of Jake and the daisy crown I wore at our wedding by White Rock Lake. Mom and Jake argued politics every time they were in the same vicinity, much less the same room. "You've got a goddamned cold heart," she'd say to end every argument. Now he absolutely has a cold heart – in fact, a cold everything. Maybe that's what getting one's reward is all about. Maybe Jake is who Mom saw in the corner, once again divining what I cannot.

I slip the crystal-stemmed glasses into their case in my purse so I can see clearly the ridiculous material my daughter insists on.

Angry, I intend to replace the lenses with my own prescription. I'm glad I insisted on taking them for myself. I think of them as mine now, but they will always be hers.

Memoir by Trajectory:
Some Quotes Concerning Fear
from the Mental Jabbering of Tabitha's Mind
as She Navigates Repeated Threats to Her
Very Well-Being

Boogie-Man's behind my closet door by the corner. I'm sure of it 'cause he's wiggling.

That tall woman in front of the blackboard isn't Mommy but she's telling me what to do. Why did my mommy leave me here?

Father Hikert says God can see everything. Oh no… Mommy says it's true and I bet she knows about Woolworth's.

Judy might speak to me in the hall. If not, I'm going to die.

If I don't make an A+ on that test I won't pass and Daddy will soooooo ground me then Jed will ask out Tara then my life will be over.

Close the door, goddammit. What if Mom smells this stuff?

Dear God, don't let me be pregnant.

Oh no ... what is that blood? I'm losing the baby.

Please God, people are already in the pews; let him show up. I hope this white satin won't show armpit stains.

Banks *have* to let you borrow money. How should they know whether we can afford it?

Oh God, let me finally have a baby.

Please please please make her understand she has to go potty before preschool starts next month.

That damn husband of mine won't tell me where the hell he's been.

Nothing matters except we save our daughter.

I saw her sip wine at Christmas dinner. Does that mean she's relapsed?

Have I done everything I can? Oh dear God, have I?

So far away she's moved!

Surely this isn't all there is?

Doctor, it was always supposed to be *me* first.

If Hospice will make it easier for you honey … but I want to be the one who takes care of you. I need to be. Of course I don't mind it. Don't mind anything, really. So … okay … I guess they can come. If you really want them.

Oh my God, that hole is squared off; it's so deep. So dark inside.

This pew feels beyond empty.

Good grief, what is that pain in my gut!

How fast it's all gone by!

Boogie-Man is definitely in the corner there but he doesn't look like what I remember. He looks a little like Jake, but Jake's dead. Oh my God, he's coming out now. He's here now. His face isn't nearly as bad as I thought it would be. Maybe he's not mean. Maybe he's nice. Kind. Ah …ah….ah….

Glamorous Bitch

LULA'S GRANDMOTHER, JUJU, possessed the classic symmetrical features that ended up in museum paintings, but she also was endowed with a well-honed skill for the perfectly-timed, mean-spirited comment which illuminated the recipient's deepest weakness. For example, when Lula had toddlers, JuJu looked around her living room and waved her hand. "Well, housework always was your weakness. Indeed any kind of work at all."

The agreed-upon reality of the extended family, however, was that Lula was JuJu's favorite grandchild of all seven. JuJu threw elaborate family birthday parties for her, and showered her with everything any little princess could want: expensive school dresses and an add-a-pearl necklace, twin Barbie dolls with multiple changes of elegant clothes and an unlimited supply of movie magazines. When Lula was a child, JuJu provided Lula with a two-week respite from Lula's annoying horrible brothers. Juju would drive up in her Cadillac and then deliver Lula to the local dimestore at which Juju allowed Lula to pick out anything she wanted to entertain herself. Lula slept under JuJu's pink linen bedspread and, when she awoke at whatever time suited her, JuJu, in her silk kimono, cut up however many strawberries Lula wanted. As the knife hit the countertop, Lula distracted JuJu with renditions of the rumors at school or the plots of movies she'd seen. Lula described in detail the expressions of all the actors and the scenes from the stories she'd read in her language arts class. JuJu's favorite word was 'glamorous.'

Time passed and the annual vacations ceased, Lula's boyfriend was accompanied down the aisle, her toddlers were delivered, and new jobs were obtained in a neighboring state. JuJu turned eighty and Lula's mother took charge of JuJu's care when such care was accepted. Lula hadn't been home in a year.

She knocked at the door of JuJu's apartment. No one appeared at the door for several minutes but when she appeared, JuJu held the door open only inches with a white-knuckled arthritic fist.

"Hello, JuJu." Lula expected an especially snide comment about her twelve-month absence. Instead, JuJu smiled gently. "How are you dear?" JuJu seemed shorter, hunched as if she could not stand up straight.

"May I come in JuJu? Have a little visit? I'm here from Arkansas."

"No dear, not today." She kept the door hiding her frame with only her head and part of her torso showing. She actually kept smiling but with an expression Lula could only think of as 'sugary.' Lula had never seen such a look on JuJu before and would never have imagined attributing it to her.

Lula softly argued a bit. "Surely you can visit for just a minute?"

"No. No, dear. Not today." She began to shut the door. "Thanks for coming by."

"But Juju," Lula tried to insert her hand into the closing door. "I'm only in town for a few days."

"Next trip, then. I love you, honey." Juju's protestations of love shocked and worried Lula. But perhaps JuJu was actually nice because her apartment was dirty or she hadn't had a bath. Or it could've been because she'd been drinking as she'd been wont to do before Lula's grandfather died. Then again perhaps she'd taken up prayer, and didn't want it to be interrupted. But the last Lula knew, JuJu was a lapsed Catholic who threw things at the TV when those Catholic bishops were accused.

No conclusion came to Lula. She asked her mother. "She's turned sweet, Lula. Just turned sweet."

"I thought people got meaner when they got old. Disappointment, regret, resentment … that kind of thing. I would've thought taking care of JuJu would've been a downright nightmare."

"She's no trouble at all, Lula. Once I told her she couldn't live with your father and me, she just little by little became … how can I say it: mysteriously pleasant? At first I thought she was manipulating us to move over here but evidently not. She's never mentioned it again."

A week later, and before Lula returned to her kids, Lula's mother discovered JuJu dead next to her bed. Among her things were a soft blue silk caftan with navy flowers and a coffee stain on it, a bottle of vodka seven-eighths full, a novel with a broken spine opened on the table next to the bed with the pink bedspread. The *Breviary* topped a stack on the floor beside the front door, as if somehow waiting to leave. Tucked inside, marking the Prayer for the Dying, was a hand-written note dated January 14, 1957, the year Lula was eight. The note said: "Thank you for everything, Judith, especially the use of your typewriter." Lula thought: I guess she wasn't mean to everyone except me.

She found the typewriter on the top of JuJu's walk-in closet underneath an unstable hat box which was empty except for roach droppings and a round brass medal on a striped cord: the Lincoln Medal for Literary Excellence. Underneath was McFall High School 1917. The typewriter was light pink, and portable. The "I" key on the typewriter stuck.

No one sells typewriter ribbons anymore, but Lula took the funny pink machine just the same. The machine was awkward and she had no idea where she'd put it or how she would keep it from her children, but she didn't seem to have any choice. It was hers.

Genius

THE PERSON ALWAYS wanted to be a genius. Having been given a greater-than-average intelligence, though not intimate experience with it, she was thrown into special classes at school and even achieved advanced degrees of one kind and another, all attempts to find that 'special gift' that defines. Maybe the person even knew some people with unexplainable abilities: someone with a photographic memory perhaps, or an unmeasurable I.Q., who could deduce econometric equations analyzing problems the general public doesn't even know exist. Maybe the person fantasized that one day, even when she was as old as thirty-one, her own ability would finally appear: full-blown and thrillingly strange and powerful, as in a dream at dawn.

The person may have heard rumors that the econometric genius, at age nineteen, threw a refrigerator across the room at a teacher while doing postgraduate research at a major university. The teacher is now paralyzed from the waist down and the econometric genius is committed to a mental hospital. The person wonders how that could possibly work out. When she dated *that* genius, he often said he could predict what any head-shrinks would say before they said it.

A doctor places a baby-boy in the person's arms. She looks into the child's eyes and although she'd always heard that when a child is born, the universe shifts, it doesn't shift for her. Instead the person is thrust into something like a war: one side in this war demands that her son be a genius and the other side insists that he never throw a refrigerator.

Time passes. The husband of the person is as steady as rain. He goes to work and brings home money so the person can enrich the baby-boy's mental capacity, a goal to which all are committed. The person becomes quite skilled at enriching. She studies books and magazine articles about the developing brain. During Baby-Boy's naptime, the person polishes up the required reading and completes all the chores that go along with enriching but then doesn't know what to do with the leftover minutes before Baby-Boy awakens. She recognizes that another child is impossible because she wakes exhausted every morning and cannot force her mind to cease preparing for Baby-Boy's future.

The person happens upon information about the transition into kindergarten. She flirts with home-schooling but her doctor tells her that if she doesn't get some sleep she'll be throwing refrigerators so she enrolls Baby-Boy into a local church's preschool. The teacher is pert, blonde, and probably incompetent, but even husband says Baby-Boy must enroll, so the person tells herself that she'll make up the lost learning by allocating more nap time minutes to reading classics to him and also by ensuring Mozart plays while she's cooking organic diners without red meat.

The incompetent teacher calls at the end of the first week. "Your child is drawing in a very unusual way," she says. The person panics; she'd been sure she knew everything about Baby-Boy. The teacher continues. "He replicates exactly everything he sees. Perfect scale, even perfect perspective. I've never seen a child draw like this."

The person doesn't know how she could possibly have missed such a thing. The teacher says he only draws with his left hand and guilt descends like an avalanche. So that's the reason her intuition has been bothering her so much lately: she didn't realize Baby-Boy was left-handed. Always, she had put blocks, crayons, and toys into his right hand. Baby-Boy will probably be throwing refrigerators before he starts elementary school. Her concern must reveal itself because the teacher says, "It's nothing to worry about. He's just fine in every way. Like all the other children, except for the drawing." The person bristles.

The person hurries to the local bookstore, having left Baby-Boy with husband just for an hour. She purchases parents' guides on left-handedness and overpriced tomes with color prints of famous paintings. On an impulse she buys a book titled *Inner Lives of Artists* and, with guilt niggling, a *Vogue* magazine. She comes home to find Baby-Boy cuddled next to husband on the couch watching *Monday Night Football.* The *Vogue* flits through her mind and she considers letting her husband handle the rest of the evening. Instead she whisks up Baby-Boy who only reaches back for husband for a few seconds. "I've got a treat for you from the bookstore," she says and Baby-Boy smiles.

At the kitchen table, she sits Baby-Boy on her lap and they flip through the book of paintings. He says "Don't WANT to look. Gimme MY crayons!" The house rule is: no coloring after dinner. Reading Time until Bath Time. But the person relents, sharpens a blue crayon and puts it into his left hand. She watches in amazement as Baby-Boy copies exactly a painting by Mary Cassatt from the book. Afterward, he giggles, throws the paper on top of the book and says, "Jason likes football and soccer, not reading. What's soccer?"

The person contains her confusion so as to avoid instilling insecurity and the next day volunteers for playground duty. She notices that Jason Lambert's mother is signed up for Wednesdays. After the first week, she begins to experience real rage at the incompetent teacher. Doesn't teacher notice how often Baby-Boy plays by himself on the swings? He seldom talks to the other boys, no matter that this person has bought him jeans just like the other boys wear or that she invites them over one at a time to ensure social development? How can a teacher not interrupt Jason Lambert's snitty little jibes: "He draws like a sissy?"

Before the end of the first semester, the teacher (without the person's knowledge) calls upon art experts. These experts make an appointment with the person and her husband. The experts want to do tests, they say, and offer opportunities. The person allows the tests and the opportunities, but goes to shrinks to make sure Baby-Boy won't throw refrigerators. The shrink tells the person to get a life and she stalks out but does take up Shear and Schnit for Fun and for Profit, which she found at the local craft store. The little scissors nip the heavy paper often and well, but no genius is revealed.

During playground duty, the person stands next to Jason Lambert's mother who talks about Jason's burgeoning soccer career and how critical it is for children to play in groups. The person blurts out, "You are so very correct; it is critical to develop our boys' special abilities. Of course, early *artistic* genius has to be fostered by adults that care about them, not other children, else the opportunity is lost forever. My Baby-Boy works with Dr. Santos at the college."

Jason Lambert's mother doesn't answer. Instead she reaches out to catch the prettiest little girl in the class who tripped on her designer skirt while scrambling up the jungle-gym and almost falling onto the pebbled ground.

That afternoon in the car, Baby-Boy says, "Mrs. Lambert made it so Pretty Girl didn't break her neck and get dead." Baby-Boy yawns. "Mommy, after naptime, can we draw from the book. Or you can cut things and I can draw you doing it. Then we can put it on the refrigerator and Daddy can see it. Can we, Mommy? The person looks in the rearview mirror. Baby-Boy's eyes are circled with a grayish tone, but he must sleep in his car seat during the drive to art lessons.

During spring break, husband is contacted by a New York agent who heard rumors of Baby-Boy's productions, which husband carefully does not call genius. The agent wants to sell Baby-Boy's drawings to collectors and manage what he is certain will be a career like Picasso's. This will require scheduling Baby-Boy every day, at a set time, to produce art for the gallery, and also increasing the time Baby-Boy spends with the somber-eyed Dr. Santos across town at the college. "Maybe we do have a prodigy," husband says. "He seems to love it, doesn't he? That makes him … well…him. Seems like a lot of work though, for you both. You know him best. You've done such a great job, achieved so much with him. Do you think we should make sure he goes for it?"

The person sets aside the little lap desk on which she sheer and schnits, begins to flip through the most recent *Vogue*: yearning yearning yearning. "Over my dead body," she answers.

Initiations
Grand Canyon Quartet

1.

Wide-spread fingers hold us back.

Dad stands on the lip of the South Rim,

> Points one finger over air toward pink, gray and brown
> stripes opposite: so far so far so far.

"One day, boys," he says, "we'll hike from here to there."

For one moment, I take in his testosterone-fueled confidence,

then punch my brother's arm.

"I'll throw you over," I say,

and he answers in kind.

2.

Time passes.

I learn to wield the poles. Better than my brother.

We graduate from one and a half mile mini-hikes to half-way
there and back.

I learn to walk and rest and push myself till finally my own
testosterone kicks in.

I grow rich; much richer than my sibling.

For a moment, I look up to see the star-filled sky,

> book the honeymoon suite;

> marry my girlfriend,

> kiss her full on her lipsticked mouth.

3.

My brother and I did hike Rim to Rim,

> but not with Dad.

> He stroked and didn't lose everything;

> hiking, however, is out.

We offer the mule deer.

"Not the same," he says.

Now he stands on the Canyon's edge.

> I spread my fingers on my son's shoulders.

Dad points to the colored stripes.

> "One day," he says, "you'll hike this crevasse in the earth."

His lip trembles.

4.

In empty minutes, I wonder if

> they felt the life-force leaving them.

Now I face the striped boulders across the expanse,

> urns in my pack.

I've hiked long enough to bear the extra weight

> and do without the extra nourishment.

At the trailhead, the sun is high.

111

I step alone.

> My wife doesn't love this,
>
> But even if she did, everyone's hike is entirely their
>
> own.

Midway at Phantom Ranch, I verify solitude,

empty the dust … say no words, cry no tears.

> Just like a grown-up man.

The smallest part of me, the grizzled hormone-part, is thankful
that my ashes

aren't the ones mixing with the Canyon's dirt,

that I am the one left standing.

Except … now at sunset …

I look up at the burgeoning Milky Way.

Nothing much separates me from those emerging lights:

> so close so close so close.

My fingers reach to click my headlamp.

And I find myself pointing toward the rocks slowly graying.

In one instant the world is still.

In one instant I am within the night,

> And only halfway home.

III.

CHOOSE

MAKING HARD CHOICES ISN'T SELF-HELP IN A BOOKSTORE.

Stamp

DARK, OF COURSE, but light illuminated from the parking lot filtered through the cheap grass shades when Jennifer got home from her class. It was 10:30 after all. She stopped outside when she left her car to relish the full, silver-white moon. She was pretty sure that, although she didn't know that boy-man's name, for the rest of her life she would link the memory of that moon with the remembrance of his rosemary breath, of his rough fingers laced with hers.

Such a quick connection after a normal, routine stop at the mailbox on Fifth Street. Jennifer hadn't even noticed him walking up at the same time as she did. Always after her class, she felt an adrenaline rush to get her day over with, her duties checked off the list she planted in her head, just to keep her world afloat. Yet when she arrived in front of the mailbox, there he was. "Slow gets it all done," he said.

She startled. Of course she did. Stopped immediately at such an intimate statement. They stood for a moment, looking at each other. He leaned over, gentle and sure, pressed his dry lips against hers. The moonlight seemed to force everything to clarity.

Absence of light in the apartment helped her deception as she stepped on her husband's trousers, almost certainly oil-stained from the garage. She made herself nude as always, then she gingerly, expertly lifted the sheet that covered his snoring frame and her empty spot next to him. She crawled into their bed, turned her back to him. She curled into a tight little s-shape then thought better of it. She slipped off the thin, gold-plate wedding ring which was all he could afford those years ago. She dropped it onto the side table. Light from the window bounced just a bit off the thin gold circlet, now so much duller than it was at the start. The band – smaller than a postage stamp – poised just on the edge of the table's edge, ready to fall.

Prompt from Facebook:
6 Words to Define Your Life

Unplanned pregnancy
Wrestle Meaning
Face Grave

or

Hot Night
Joy, Sorrow
Sealed Casket

or

Present
Choose
Consequence

or

Routes
Turn
Arrive

Twist

MOONLIGHT SHONE SO bright he almost felt in daylight, but the other-worldly silver illumined differently than the sun's true gold. The perfect contours of her face were slightly less distinct than the outline of her body which he felt rather than saw. First, they mapped out for the umpteenth time their plan for their lives: graduation, college, marriage, a home. Always they ignored threats. Therefore, when he entered her, he closed his eyes against any contrary vision nature might allow him, seeing in his mind only the glorious, regular relief he imagined. Despite the prediction they'd conjured by the light of what seemed a fixed moon, they missed the twist in the path before them which took them someplace else entirely.

Duty: A Study in Grammar

THERE WAS A man—just a boy, really—who did his duty.

"I'm pregnant," the blonde girl said. No one would mistake *her* for a grown woman. Her liquid blue eyes were pierced with vulnerability and strength all at the same time, a real looker who'd been damaged by crazy, alcoholic relatives in a way which only enhanced the young man's captivation. That captivation had been going on since last year, his freshman year at the local college where he read classic novels and excelled in rhetoric. He'd met her on the basketball court of his old high school. She'd slipped on a piece of ice from her Dr. Pepper.

They stood face-to-face on the corner of a street in the poor section of a rich neighborhood in a town whose name doesn't matter. It was 1948, in the spring. The day was hot, a precursor of the sweltering summer to come, and it was full daylight.

"Of course we'll get married." He spoke quickly, with a definiteness he did not entirely feel but which he knew he must choose. He had a hard time making himself do things sometimes.

No one knew about this quality in him. His handsome face belied anything but strict confidence. To every authority in his life—his parents, his teachers, the minister, his boss at the malt shop, even the rich girls who stirred up his juices—he was the golden boy, the one who would make good, the "smart" one who had what it took to get educated, make something of his handsome self. Yet with all the powers he supposedly had, the boy knew his mind was shot through with a gentle intuitive two-sidedness that weakened him somehow in a world that rewarded the brute force of undivided will.

He came to discover his weakness when he was ten, during the Bible School he attended with the kid down the street. Some Episcopal monks from out of town ran the Bible School for three weeks in the summer, a way for the church to keep their boys off the streets. The boy had been fascinated with one monk in particular and sat next to him, with his coarse brown habit, during the prayers. That monk had looked into the boy—when he was a boy—in a way and with a connection that the boy had never experienced before. The boy loved that connection and also the exploration of religious history and all the various kinds of spirituality he'd never heard of before: Buddhism and Hinduism and Monasticism. The boy felt he'd been seen as no one else had ever bothered to really see him before. The monk asked him if he was an Episcopalian. "No, I'm not," he answered. The monk shook his head and walked away; the boy felt deflated.

But the boy, though he didn't know how to explain it even to himself, ended that summer with an ethereal sense of not *fully* belonging to the regular world of schools and friends and families. Though he went about his life, a little voice in the back of his brain kept nudging him about his experience with the monk whenever he made decisions that mattered, whenever it was hard for him to make such decisions. He always knew what was expected of him, what was the *right* thing to do, but he always needed to convince himself he could find the energy to follow through with what was wanted of him.

Now, standing in front of the blonde girl was definitely one of those times, and his lack of psychic energy was worse than it had ever been. Yet he loved the blonde girl; she never bored him like the sorority girls did. He ignored the little voice jabbering in his mind while he made their plans. He dismissed the feeling that he was putting a period on the end of life as he knew it.

He reached for the Camels rolled up in the right sleeve of his white t-shirt. The religious stuff was out now, he supposed. He'd get to it later, he promised himself. Maybe something would happen. It always did—for him. He dug matches out of his dungarees, lifted his foot, and swiped the red tip against the sole of his shoe. His shoes had a weak spot, needed to be re-soled, and he had to repeat the procedure.

He borrowed money for the ring, a narrow gold band with a little pearl set as a diamond solitaire would be set. His parents didn't come to the wedding, but hers did—and they glowered at him in the dim light of the priest's office. The boy liked the office himself, despite the tension that hovered. Bookshelves stuffed with interesting titles lined the walls. When they had first asked the priest to marry them, he had made a mental note to visit again; any priest with fiction on his shelves couldn't be all bad.

Baby-girl Mae was born. He was overwhelmed by her and didn't sleep soundly for months. Every time she wiggled in the little drawer that served as a bassinet, he startled awake. When the blonde girl moved the baby to the small square area that was their 'living room,' the boy slept better. Still his daughter changed everything.

She needed a christening dress. He and the blonde girl had taken to attending the church where the priest had married them. Besides the christening dress, the blonde girl wanted to take the baby to the doctor a lot more frequently than they could afford. He was too embarrassed to ask his friends for a loan and his parents weren't speaking to him much. He abandoned his college plans, accepted the full time job his boss had been trying to force onto him. His natural friendliness and the fact that he really didn't care to manipulate his customers made him the best salesman in the place. He was promoted and got a $3-an-hour raise. Baby Mae got her christening dress and went to the best doctor in their neighborhood.

Time passed. Life was busy. The blonde girl wanted to work in one of the department stores downtown. "No," he said, "I can handle it. You should take care of Mae."

And he *did* deliver on his promise. Ten years later, they had not one, but three children—"brats" he joked, and wrestled, laughing, with all three of them at once on the floor of the now larger apartment. He bought a set of books whose publishers made the claim that reading them would substitute for a Harvard education. The books made the blonde girl mad; she needed a new divan. He would come home from the store and fall onto their old ratty couch and look at the small cherrywood-tone bookcase on the other side of the room, but he couldn't open the books yet. He was too sad and too exhausted. Instead he got a library card and read through all the Louis L'Amour.

Finally, though, he could stand the empty spot inside him no longer. He began reading the Harvard books and fights ensued. His wife needed help with the kids, she said, and he wasn't doing what he should. He got a job peddling men's underwear in South Texas. It meant more money—a great deal more—and it had the added benefit of solitude from Sunday night until Friday at five—all at someone else's expense. Surely she could cope when it really came down to it.

She could not. The vulnerability which had captivated him, and captivated him still, finally exacted its price. His absence exacerbated the situation. Her mind cracked in a way he hadn't known could even exist. He put her in a state hospital under the care of an intern psychiatrist they'd known in high school. The psychiatrist was a good man and got her well enough to come home. The boy didn't believe in raking over one's feelings. He refused to go to the doctor with her, but still the blonde girl regained being functional again. She took care of the children, and though she was a bit more intense than before, she was able to fight her demons while he was on the road. The first week that she was home and he was able to work again, he took along *An Interpretation of Dreams* from the cherry bookshelf and tucked it into his suitcase. As the boy read it, he didn't hesitate to recognize the man's genius. Although all the boy had come to understand about psychological development made perfect sense, still the realization didn't fill that funny spot in him. The boy's search continued.

When the children were in eighth, fifth, and third grades, he had a revelation. It happened when he was the volunteer superintendent of the Sunday School. He noticed there were two kinds of teachers. The majority presented highly structured lessons and were entirely sure of themselves. But the others, the minority, spent most of the class just listening to their charges. These last teachers were the ones the children loved the best and they were also the ones who ended up in the youth group.

"Why do you spend your time with them like that," he asked one of the minority,

"I like to listen," the teacher answered. "Plus if you listen, you learn something."

"Where did you get that?"

"Father Jeff is that way. I guess I got it there."

The comment struck the boy to the heart. He resigned the Sunday School job and volunteered instead to lead the Inquirer's

Class in their small living room—the room with the new, firm divan.

He loved the Inquirers. He loved everything about it: loved preparing for it, loved attending it, loved the people that came. Loved—more than anything he had ever done—connecting with the people who poured out their questions, even when he didn't have the answers which was most of the time. It was not exactly the same, but almost, like connecting to that monk he had met long ago.

Father Jeff noticed he was exceptional at the entire process. "Come to the Diocesan Retreat with us," he said.

The boy—still the victim of that psychic weakness—didn't hold back even as much as he did when he ate or slept or cleared his bowels. Never before had he answered so confidently as he did in that minute when he agreed to attend.

As he packed for the retreat, the blonde girl walked into their bedroom—scene of sex and intimacy, but not the scene of his reading. Reading, he did in the living room so she could sleep the exhausted sleep of one who never should have had children in the first place. These days he read in the house instead of a cheap motel because he had taken yet another job. Again the job was one that paid better but had the added benefit of keeping him home to help out. He missed the privacy but bore it.

The blonde girl was sullen at his packing, but less so than she used to be when he left. "Do you know where my argyle socks are?" he asked.

"Uh, no. Listen. While you're gone, we need to decide whether to let Mae try out for the drill team. It'll cost $125 for the uniform and boots and stuff. I think she needs to do it, don't you? It'd help her confidence, help her be more well-rounded. She's gotten obsessed with school this year."

He stopped packing, rubbed the side of his face where the stubble awaited his razor. He didn't think Mae was obsessed at all. School was just what she liked to do. It was unfortunate she didn't make the grades to match her ambition, but he liked that she took it all so seriously. Still, his wife was right about one thing: the child needed to get some exercise, make some friends. He himself had to have weekly tennis or he felt like the devil. "Okay. I'll just count over at Harry's for a few weekends. Tell her it's okay." Harry was a youngish friend who owned a warehouse; sometimes Harry hired extras for their monthly inventory.

"I'll do it over at Harry's," the blonde girl—now a woman—offered.

He felt the old tug inside his mind. He could let her make the money this time. He caught himself just in time, though. "Nah. I'll do it."

He was the only layman at the retreat so he was tapped to acolyte. He'd missed that duty as a child; his parents weren't religious and certainly not Episcopalian. As his hands cupped around the little silver box that held the wafers, Father Jeff smiled at him gently— a fatherly smile and the boy relaxed inside, felt that connection, felt *seen*.

After the mass, Father Jeff approached him. "Let's go for a walk."

They walked for a long time, silent in the East Texas woods, then spoke with moderated tones of which no one but those two ever knew the content. At the end of it, the boy retired to the monastic room to which he'd been assigned and there fought a battle no one could have understood. When he emerged, he left behind something of himself.

At home, he gave up teaching the Inquirers' Class. He hadn't intended to, but time pressed in on him. He worked at Harry's every Saturday, counting with the poor folks who had no education but provided him with endless stories of their struggles. The other workers found him a ready listener who made no judgments.

His regular job weighed him down less and less. He still bore the weakness but he didn't fight it as much. For a long time he turned his mind from the empty place that didn't seem to matter anymore.

Mae did not earn a place on the drill team, but she did go to college. All three of the children did. The boy, now over forty, and the blonde girl never could figure out how they'd done it.

Time passed. Within the years were five attempts to quit smoking, a daughter who got suicidal once, a son who became addicted, then got sober, and grandchildren that almost went wrong. In these middle years, he bought a business that failed and afterwards he lived through a period when all he could do was sit in an orange recliner wondering what to do for money, what he could do to pay Mae's phone bill from college. He went back to Harry's then a few times, to pay for the phone bill. Finally he went back on the road; he always could convince people to buy things. His wife did better without him around this time; she enrolled at a local community college to keep herself busy. Her confidence grew and she blossomed.

Companies that hired sales reps just weren't stable during the 70s and 80s, and he kept having to change what it was he sold, but the buyers always welcomed whatever he was pushing; they loved being around him. He and his wife discovered cheap trips to Europe where people didn't think about money so much; he loved that. Loved it so much he gave each of the kids a trip one year instead of going himself .

In the end it was the cigarettes that got him. He developed lung cancer when he was sixty-seven, a few years past the average age. He'd ignored the warning signs for awhile before, although the blonde woman, knowing something was very wrong, frantically begged him to go for tests, to fight against what she suspected was happening. The doctors said the tumor could not be removed. He made his peace but no one ever really understood how he did so. His family only noticed he got simpler and simpler as the months wore on. He got up earlier in the morning to disappear into the guest bedroom. His demeanor became increasingly child-like.

Over the years, all his children found religion—each made God their own. Their respective faiths were wildly divergent, not borrowed from anyone else. Each learned to listen to that "still small voice" that the boy—now a man—had ignored, fought against, tried to dismiss, given into, then come to love, and, finally, to rely upon. It came as no surprise to anyone except the three of them that he directed they be the pallbearers at his funeral.

Many people attended that funeral: the nurse who'd administered his chemotherapy, a few of the old black men who'd counted widgets at Harry's, Harry himself, the coffee group that met in the parish hall every Sunday after church, many of the people he'd offered his soft goods to over the years, a smattering of the college boys who'd returned to their town to start their now flourishing businesses. By then, Father Jeff was dead of old age and his replacement delivered a sermon no more than two and a half minutes, again at the boy's insistence. The blonde wife, along with everyone else, celebrated the Eucharist. The boy was buried outside of the now booming city—a city that had passed him by—

in a cemetery the boy and his wife had decided upon and they could afford. The most common statement made that day was: "I didn't know the old boy was so religious."

After all the guests had left their casseroles and flowers, hugs and encouragements, the children went back to where, with a mechanical hoe, the gravediggers pushed the dirt over the place in which his body would forever be encased.

"He would have been such a good priest," the middle child said. "It makes me sad that he never was one."

"I know," answered the son. "I wonder if he ever wanted that, ever seriously considered it?"

"But he was a priest. The whole time," said Mae, the oldest girl, the one for which the boy, now a man, did his duty.

Forms of Defiance 3:
Implied Commitments Made to the
Listener/Reader/Viewer/Other
Ignored, Broken, or Deserted
Which Are Irrelevant to the Unfolding of Real
Life

Absolutely Never Works: Preaching.

Technique Employed: Second Person or else Sly Subtext ....

No Escape from Yourself is Possible.

Chad's Room

THE CLOSET COMPANY sent someone to count her clothes. She would need the proper number of inches to hang things in the master closet she was making out of Chad's empty bedroom. The company suggested categories divided up by butternut-colored panels from ceiling to floor. The top part would house blouses and the bottom pants or skirts, with special hooks for suits and belts, a glass-fronted cupboard for sweaters.

She put her white clothes in one section and the blacks in another. Since she'd been on leave from work, she'd cut down on colors – changed her look, so to speak. She put together the "moving on" clothes she had deliberately collected in past months. But those still didn't make up the majority of what she owned.

She did the best to organize her husband's things, and asked him to help, but he mostly laid on the den couch, flipping channels and sipping. He said the closet was a useless expense— lately he said nothing was worth buying. Nothing, that is, except whiskey or back-to-back, pay-per-view movies, despite that he'd never had use for anything except the business channel; they'd had that in common. She tidied his clothes as best she could, bit her tongue.

When the wall units were finished, the closet-maker added a matching island in the center of the room—right where Chad used to hunker down and play with multi-colored Legos that matched his bedspread. The island consisted of a 4½-by-8-foot counter on top of three sets of drawers on either side. Her husband didn't even bother to put his socks in the drawers, but she utilized all of her space: in one she tucked her underwear, from which she carefully culled the ragged or provocative, and in another she arranged her jewelry. One drawer held her workout clothes—though she couldn't seem to get enough energy for that as of late.

In the bottom drawers, she put mementos: a glass chalice that had been a favor at a college dance, her high school diploma in a black plastic frame, love letters from her husband when he'd been in boot camp her senior year. In a heavy linen envelope was the commendation he'd received for leadership. Her mother's handkerchiefs, a few she used herself on special occasions such as weddings or funerals, and a set of silver-plated spoons her great grandmother had collected from vacations. In the final drawer, the one nearest the door, she placed Chad's plastic Army men, and his little rusted cars, his burnt orange baseball cap with the white longhorn stitched on the bill. There was also a math test of word problems he'd taken for Mrs. Peminta's 3rd grade class—with a huge red A+/"You've got quite a future!!!" on it. Two yellow-stained batiste rompers she'd embroidered for him, and his size six ragged blue jeans. The blue flannel shirt that matched his eyes. The plaster imprint of his hand from Sunday school. She wrapped each of these items in acid-free paper and determined not to paw through them for a long long time.

When all the pants were hung, all the blouses freshly pressed on padded hangers, all the black jackets aligned like sentries facing her, she put her hands on her hips and surveyed the result of her labors. She should have been relieved. With a leather-shoed toe, she shut the memento drawer with Chad's things. It bounced open, then was still. The memory of his bunk beds, with rumpled cowboy sheets, shimmered in front of her, and the smell of him clung to this disinfected room.

"Honey," she yelled toward the den. "Come look."

He didn't come until she'd called him three times, then came up behind her, put his heavy palm on her shoulder. The despised plaid robe fell open. He hadn't showered in days. She leaned against him anyway, and sighed.

An Exercise in Memory
for the Non-Homeless and Especially Those Laboring Women Whose Contractions Have Shrunk to under Two Minutes Apart

'This is the automated Early Warning Emergency Blackboard of the Town of Highland Park. The National Weather Service has issued a Severe Thunderstorm Warning for Dallas, Collin, and Tarrant Counties, which includes our area.

Take cover immediately.

Winds are expected to be 50-60 miles per hour. During a Severe Thunderstorm, tornadoes can develop with very little warning.

Take cover immediately in the safest place within your home, either a central hallway or in an enclosed bathtub in the lower level of your home. Cover yourself with mattresses or other padding if you are able.

Stay away from windows.

Do not drive. Flash flooding is expected along all major highways and roads going into and out of the Town of Highland Park. Be aware that heavy winds can damage power lines.

This warning will be in effect until 8:45 p.m.

Take cover immediately.

Press * to repeat this message.

Press 2 to be removed from the Early Warning Emergency Blackboard.

Press 3 to speak with the Town Tax Collection Department.

Press 4 to be connected to the Waste Management Team.

Press 5 to speak to the Police Department.

Press 6 for directions to the Town Hall.

Press star to repeat this message.

Press star to repeat this message.

Press star to repeat this message.

Learning to Write: Divergence Gets Slippery

THE PROFESSOR WON the Teacher of the Year Award for 2001, so it was a surprise when he opened this class with: "Okay, here's an exercise that's going to tell you all you need to know about writing stories. Just two parts. First, write your name. Second, write your alias."

I wrote my name: Cynthia Anne Croan Parrett Sample Whatever. This was a family joke made by my husband, John, because Croan is my maiden name, my first husband's name was Charles Parrett, Sample became my name after Charles died and I married John, and John claimed I would surely marry someone else after him so what would that man's name be? *Whatever.* That's the joke, see, my name, but that is in fact my name now since John died just a few years ago, even if I haven't found Mr. Whatever.

I was proud of this first step in the exercise and looked forward to telling it to the class, but of course now this first part makes what follows a memoir. It's nothing that could lead to a story like a fairy tale or a magazine romance or some novel at the grocery store. I became a different character every time I added a new last name.

I turned my attention to coming up with aliases: Abigail Mae Marten, Anne Florence Blakely, Blakely Hauser, Blakely Kellogg, Blake Posden, Blakely Mae Berry, John Summerville, Alex Blake, Alex Charles. None of these satisfies me at all. They are just syllables on the page and every one of them has some connection to my real life or the people I'm from. Maybe that's because I have so many weird relatives: eccentric, dysfunctional, or downright silly. 'Course, I'm Southern so that's to be expected. Or perhaps I simply have no imagination.

None of these aliases seems to be half as interesting as my own real family or even my own history, so I choose Alex Blake because after all I want to pass this class. Just being named Blake instead of Blakely like my grandmother doesn't make this process any less messy. Uncertainty is slippery: if names have any real flesh on them, then nothing is really totally apart from the one that sets things down. Even my name isn't the same concrete as it was yesterday or the day before or the day before that or even tomorrow, husbands aside. After all, I'm making it all up anyway. Even with the facts, those marks on the page are just what I decide to reveal.

Big Bend

MY HUSBAND INSISTS on adventures. So here I am: packing for a place I know about in theory, not in fact. My prayer-time literature fits into the bottom of a new black duffle bag: my Bible, two daily devotionals, and *The Imitation of Christ*, which I'm reading for Lent. My purse is big enough for the trade paperbacks I'm working through: Nouwen, O'Connor, Merton, and Lewis.

"Why are you taking all that?" He folds shirts and shorts made of drab parachute-like fabric and tucks them into his own well-worn duffle bag. Something bright-colored emerges from a paper sack in his hand. "For you!" Women's versions of his shirts, but in turquoise and red, a pair of pants that fit me perfectly in charcoal grey—these have zip-off legs to make shorts. "In case we get hot on our hikes," he explains. He produces a nylon holder with a belt loop. "For water. Need it on the trails."

I yank the tags off the clothes, fold them on top of the books. "I forgot to get a camera," I say. Who wants to be recorded looking like a fool?

"What's new?" He laughs, continues to fold, and tuck. "It's okay. We'll get a disposable on the way. That way we can share the trip with the girls. You could take notes even, do a travel journal sort of a thing. We really are going at the perfect time. Davis says the foliage should be in bloom now. Not too cool; not too hot. Desert and mountains—you're going to love Big Bend. Too bad the girls won't go."

137

I'm always trying to give religion to our two prodigal reprobates, and here he is, proposing travelogues, but the Bible speaks of nature teaching about God, so I retrieve a blank spiral notebook from a bottom drawer. Maybe I can insert Bible verses or quotes or something.

The prodigals think of God as a kind of gas—vaguely infecting everything, even rocks. Certainly not how I understand God. When I refer to Him speaking to me, they talk about brain chemistry. If I should mention a passage from the Bible, they hold up their palm to me and shake their head. I know my attitude is controlling —wrong even: they're adults. But despite theology, the fact is I'm superstitious. If they don't find God before I die, *then* what'll happen to them? Not to mention *their* children, who remain unbaptized. My daughters refuse church, and recently even made an issue of prayer before family meals. I try hard to fight this obsession of mine. I read self-help books, and attempt various strategies of communication. I pray and meditate and repeat affirmations all the time. My husband's answer is to get my mind off it.

So here we are, packing. I've surrendered, am willing to try it his way. Still, I pull up the hiking clothes to make sure I've got *The Imitation of Christ*. Our chattering mutes as the miles pile up on the way south and west. I try to catch up on my reading and, with occasional glimpses when I look away from Henri Nouwen, see the landscape morph from oak-lined residential to mesquite-studded ranches to whitish dirt dotted with cacti. Mountains appear to have popped up out of flatland. The second day, we dress in our parachute clothes, sneakers, water bottle holsters. Though I need mental protection, my devotional time is cut short; my husband says we must beat the heat. His gun slips into a pocket, a knife into a small holster that fits onto his belt, power bars. He's ready for any eventuality. What is he expecting? An escapee from Huntsville Prison, or a mama bear separated from her cubs? At the Visitors Center he buys a map and a trail guide. The Lost Mine Trail is our first hike: five miles to the top and out again—further than I've walked at one time since I was a child.

The trail is only slightly uphill at the beginning. I think: I can do this. A birding club walks within earshot ahead of us. One guy's voice filters through the vegetation, and he refers, over and over, to his vacation home in Maine. He describes the national park there, and talks with a rat-ta-tat voice about how Rockefeller designed every single rock-hewn step, the lining of every path, exactly what guests would see. It's hard to think about the path while imagining an entirely different place. We zigzag up our mountain, each zag getting shorter, each zig getting steeper. I slip on the gravel early on—maybe I don't have the proper shoes after all?—and thereafter keep my eyes on the path, never really too narrow, regularly enhanced with hewn steps, but anxiety-producing anyway.

The birding group stops regularly, and we pass them, then they pass us, then we pass them. "Hurry," my husband says, and I huff and puff to do so. Some kind of bird makes himself hoarsely, hauntingly known, even amidst the wind in the trees. "In the Acadia Park, that'd be a loon," the Maine birder says, and I wonder what a loon truly sounds like and I imagine different trees. I stumble and refocus on the walkway ahead of me. "Drink up," my husband reminds me and I lift and sip. I put out one foot after the other, struggle to the bare red boulder at the top of the trail. It's said that, if there's clear air, a person can sometimes see 142 miles from that spot. The wind has died down, and it does seem as if we see a long long way ... but 142 miles? I squint, blink, squint again . . . a fuzzy outline of bumps that might be mountains through a haze. No specifics, though, like trees or trails or even a firm outline. Is that seeing?

The birders catch up. One pulls out binoculars, and focuses through the trees. "Look there," he points. "That funky rock over there. It's like a totem pole. Can we get to it?" My husband and I take turns peering through our own binoculars, but I dismiss the strange rock—there are so many formations. Who needs totem poles? I have enough gods to figure out.

The walk down the mountain feels easier, but still, I am sore when we reach our hotel. The night sky is translucent and a hotel clerk tells us the McDonald Observatory nearby will host a stargazing party. We dress in long pants, but even with my jacket hood tied tightly under my chin, I shiver in the forum-shaped outdoor theater. A graduate student tells us what we are seeing as we crane our necks, teaches us the order of the heavens: Big Dipper, Little Dipper, North Star. The group hustles out, back down the hill toward the central building where the telescopes are situated. My husband stands in line to peer through the largest telescope. With the expense mentioned, I'm surprised there is more than one. I peer at Saturn through one of the smaller telescopes. Saturn looks just like a picture in a library book except the image is whiter than white. I withdraw and scurry toward the café and cocoa.

I wait for my husband in a small movie theater with gray flannel seats, and sip my cocoa as I watch a documentary that attempts to explain distance to me so I can understand a quasar, newly discovered and 12.7 billion light years away. The film begins with a family picnicking in a Midwestern park—the children wear brightly colored play clothes and chase bugs in the grass while the mother stashes leftover lunch in a basket and the father falls asleep. The camera pulls back over and over again, each time showing the viewer what the universe looks like from that imagined vantage point. Soon, I'm seeing white dots on a black background in the shape of the Milky Way, then the camera seems to rush back down down down, and the white dots become larger and larger, until finally color appears on the children's clothes and their parents are doing what parents do. The camera moves to focus on a green blade of grass, ever closer, detailing what it's made of. The documentary explains, again with camera tricks, the relative size of protons and neutrons and quarks. By the time my husband sits next to me with his own cocoa, I'm dizzy and confused and longing to get to my bed.

We are first to shove through the glass doors and I hug myself as I shake in the cold wind and look up. Maybe I could bring the grandchildren here. The vastness of the universe, and the delicacy of its balance, could say a lot. There's Scripture on that.

The next morning, we persist and tackle another trail. We zigzag again into Santa Elena Canyon where schoolchildren yell into the river-space between the boulders past which no one can see; listen for the world to speak back to them. I try it myself, only I don't yell "Elvis is alive," or "Go Panthers" or even "Jesus Saves." Compelled, I yell my name, and the sound reverberates back to me in ever-decreasing waves. Soon, the sound dissipates to nothing, and the wind ceases blowing for a moment, yet the emptiness remains with sunlight glinting.

Afterwards, I gather up the guidebooks and brochures and the still-empty spiral notebook and bend to throw them on the bottom of my duffle. The disposable camera gets tucked between the now-wrinkled parachute shirts without any descriptive journal of our experience—words have defied me.

At home, I develop the pictures, try and fail again to describe what our trip was like. My husband had photographed, but I fix up the album—a black vinyl thing from the pharmacy. The prodigals bring casseroles to welcome us home. After dinner, I sit with them on each side of me, our thighs touching in a little hill-like line. The un-baptized grandbabies grab at everything within reach and shake the bars of the babygate that confines them to the den. I find myself talking about stargazing and Rockefeller, then interrupt my travelogue for safety's sake. "Honey, no," I say to the baby.

"Were there flowers?" one prodigal asks.

I pull a brochure out from between the pages. "See here: 'Vegetation of the Desert.' Desert marigold. Prickly pear cactus. Octillo. Rock nettle and Torrey yucca."

The littlest baby-girl crumples a magazine between sticky fingers; she laughs at the sound of it, her eyes intent. I lean over, crumple it into a ball once I wrest it from her. I'm fearful the ink will muss her pink sun-dress, or worse, poison her somehow.

"But how did they smell? Did you pick any?" My daughter seems oblivious to the danger. I sit down, keep my eyes on the child.

"I think I saw some. I was so busy putting one foot in front of the other. It was really steep and I kept slipping. And there were all these people behind us—birders from Maine that wouldn't stop talking about somewhere else." I say this as I cup the baby's soft middle, lift her into my lap.

"Describe the air up there, being at those high elevations."

I'm unable to formulate an answer. The baby cries in despair; her entire self is consumed with the loss of the magazine. No baptismal anxieties for her.

My daughter takes the baby from me, wiggles her fingers for distraction. I take my car keys from my pocket, and hand them over. She speaks. "At least tell me what you liked most."

"The main thing I remember from the trip was Santa Elena Canyon, but it's hard to tell about. Maybe you just have to go there yourself. I yelled my name through the mountains, over the river. See the picture of it, there?" I point to the brochure. "Anyway, there was this outcropping over the Rio Grande that you could stand on—and I yelled my name. An echo came back, even in the wind. You know the Bible talks about the Holy Spirit being like wind."

Both prodigals roll their eyes. "Lay off, Mother."

I do lay off, and smile at littlest baby-girl. But I think of the wind through all those trees, how it sounded like something else but the words to explain it are still just out of reach. Like marbles jostling against one another? Like water trickling over stones? Truth just underneath consciousness as I tried and tried to avoid falling to my knees in the gray gravel put there by human hands.

Talent

I WANT TO be Eudora Welty but there are impediments. Although I do love my mother, I am certain I cannot live with her even if I could have an upstairs bedroom. Plus I really despise camellias and could not envision myself tending to thirty-five varieties of them. Also I do not possess a gaggle of friends to pal around with. I do not have any famous friends such as Katherine Anne Porter or Reynolds Price, although I do enjoy their stories. I do not play bridge and even if I did, I would miss the local club on occasion. I gag when drinking cocktails even at the right hour. Also I do not live in Jackson, Mississippi, or even the Deep South. Finally, I am not tall.

Mental Illness

So hard to be crazy.

But easier than life.

A Metafictional Reality: A Tale of Metaphysics

THE WIFE SITS in a green vinyl chair next to Husband's mechanical bed in the Oncology ward of Baylor University Research Hospital. Poison drips into his arm; professionals call it medicine. She snaps shut *Selected Stories of Alice Munro*; the sound is like a snowball thudding against the glass, its flakes flying this way and that when the snowball hits. Husband almost wakes up.

She wants to redirect her mind away from Mundane Sadness, but she's already read her book and all the magazines and so decides to become a Storyteller to entertain herself. The nurse shows up dressed in her blue cotton uniform. "Life-giving chemo," the nurse calls the poison as she checks the intravenous line, flicks her fingernail on the clear plastic connectors. Of course, everyone knows the poison isn't life-giving at all, not at Stage 4. Chemo just dances around death with increasing futility. The whole place smells like urine and is somnolent and heavy and silent. The Wife should be sleepy too, but she's strung tight like barbed wire around an interminable landscape that feels beige as hell. Does she want anything, Nurse asks? Yes, Wife-now-Storyteller answers, I want some paper. Nurse finally leaves with a smile and returns with the paper, seeming deeply relieved she can do something concrete.

Wife-now-Storyteller digs in the huge purse she thought would contain all she would want today but which, obviously, does not, since it does not contain enough distractions from The Situation. The purse was expensive and she carries it regularly these days because it has lots of pockets for things they need as they travel from waiting room to waiting room. While Husband snores, she licks the lead of the pencil that's been at the bottom of her purse since before The Diagnosis.

She taps the pencil against her teeth. So, she thinks, which is the more interesting point of view? The Spouse who takes the high road all her life and gets to stand in regal black at the funeral, or the Mistress nobody acknowledges? The Wife would ignore the Mistress who showed up at the funeral wearing a red silk dress, approaching the Wife as if she were some stranger instead of being intimately tied to her. In this story, the Wife should know all about this Mistress—the Wife being the one who pays the bills and, after all, how can a woman miss something like that unless she wants to? Unless somehow it's to her benefit to miss it. Or else she's just not experienced enough to know about such things. Of course, in that case, the Wife wouldn't be the one to pay the bills.

It is absolutely critical to be interesting. Maybe it would be *more* interesting if the protagonist was the Mistress getting dressed in a one bedroom apartment subsidized by Husband who is dying. Indeed who at this point would be already dead, though the Mistress would hardly know it since, being the Mistress, she wouldn't have seen the Husband through the last horrible ordeal. She wouldn't have smelled death or changed diapers or cried herself to sleep every night in fear of the cataclysm about to overtake. Indeed that ordeal that's banging on their home's door every second. How would this particular Mistress find out about the funeral in the first place? Newspaper? A call from a fellow Mistress? Maybe just Husband's unexpected absence for weeks on end?

Maybe all that's required of the Mistress is to run her fingers through some cold jewelry nestled in a black velvet box with one hand while she drums on her dresser with the painted nails of the other hand? Those jewels are probably fake; this is something the high-road Wife might have figured out since she pays those bills. One-of-Many-Mistresses might just stand there naked and struggle to decide if she should show up at the funeral at all. She might be afraid to attend, say good-bye, but long to do so. Finally she might decide she will sit at the back of the church; she's sure which one it is most likely to be because Husband was, after all, a leader there and confessed that to her once, his voice dripping with guilt but without conviction. No one need know who she is; she could be some random secretary. What would it matter anyway if high-road-Wife knew about her now that it's all over?

Maybe all the Mistress has to do is slip on the red silk dress, stand in line with everyone else to console the Wife, who by now is dressed in black-knit widow's weeds appropriate to The Occasion. The Mistress might have a mascara-streaked face and not look young anymore, but the Wife—who takes the high road most of the time—keeps her face as immobile as she can, even with the tip-off of the red silk dress. She might just stand in the receiving line and wish she could write another story instead of this one that has a life of its own.

Indian Blanket

CHAMP, YOUR FAVORITE-EVER English setter, lies curled up on his ratty Indian blanket next to the den couch. Your best friend Roland, before he died, was the one who taught you: at the first, you feel a lump. So when you reach down to rub the side of Champ's face and he lifts his red-spotted head and, with watery brown eyes, pulls away, you're alarmed. You don't remember him ever doing that. "Hey, Champ, what *is* that?" Is it a warning or are you just being womanish?

You need to get your mind off this kind of stuff. Plus, it's a good day to head out to the ranch, but it takes some preparation. You swab the inside of your shotgun's barrel with the cleaning rod and wipe the outside with gun oil and the little fabric square you're always losing. You keep getting distracted thinking about Roland and his awful dying; you wish you had been able to help him or even his wife out of it.

Rose Anne walks in, her arms full of packages from the mall. "Grady, why the hell do you keep *doing* that on the Oriental rug?" Her packages fall to the den floor, then she starts wadding up the paper towels you use to set your supplies on. It feels like a religious ritual.

"Grady, did Dr. Jackson call about your PSA test?" Her nagging contorts her forehead into grooves.

"Nope," you lie. "Champ here been to the vet lately?" The words are empty of rancor, but her lips tighten anyway. Recently you read that the longer couples stay together, the more irritated they get with each other; this surprised the researchers because studies showed that people get better at handling their emotions as they grow older. You don't have much faith in science.

She rolls her eyes. "He's your dog, for Christ's sake. But no, I haven't taken him. His teeth need cleaning; his breath's been awful lately."

"Silly to clean a dog's teeth, Rose Anne."

"Not according to my dad."

Rose Anne's father took her duck hunting every Thanksgiving of her childhood. Her own camouflage hangs in the closet and her gun leans next to yours in the gun safe. As a result, she's convinced she understands English setters, ranches, and hunting. You humor her.

"He has a funny little something in his jaw. Right here." You reach down to touch him again. This time, when Champ yanks his head away, he whimpers. Last night he didn't clean out his bowl.

Rose Anne steps over the packages, tries to caress Champ's head with both palms, but he pulls his head away from her, then looks up into her eyes.

"Maybe you shouldn't take him out this time. Sam takes his Lab."

How could someone be married to you for twenty-four years and not remember you hate the way Sam's Lab steps in front of other dogs to flush when he shouldn't?

When you get to the field, Champ jumps out of the truck slower than usual. God, what a dog: he was *born* broke! You bragged to Sam and Roland that the first time Champ was in the field, he pointed perfectly, he never had to be taught to come when called

150

or even taught not to move in ahead of hunters. Sam's Lab jumps around like a puppy though he's full-grown. You miss Roland and his pointers.

Once you and Sam start out, Champ seems normal; maybe you're just imagining things about that lump because of what's going on in your own body. Champ stands stock-still as you walk up behind him, shotgun at the ready. A little breeze feathers the tip of his tail. You lift your gun; the covey flushes. You shoot, miss. Goddamn. Goddamn old-age eyes.

Later that night, the sheets rustle as Rose Anne puts her palm on your hip bone. "Dr. Jackson's office should've called by now."

You haven't told her because it wasn't necessary. Let her live in a little ignorance, like you're trying to do. You don't have to go back to Dr. Jackson til next Tuesday, til you're off your aspirin for a few days. Why live a bad day twice?

You turn your back to her, sense her body tensing. "Talk to me," she says. "I can tell something's wrong."

"Let it go, Rose Anne. The doctor said nothing much. Go to sleep. Take Champ to the vet."

She's silent for a moment, doesn't snuggle or insist. "You do it. I've got a hair appointment tomorrow. He's probably fine."

On Tuesdays, Rose Anne gives in and cooks eggs. Eggs get a bad rap, you've argued, eggs a few times a week couldn't hurt anyone. "Eggs give you heart attacks," she insists. She used to try to fool you with substitutes, or give you pancakes, or a fancy cereal she made herself. Nowadays, she makes omelets, but with her lips pursed.

On Monday night, you sneak Champ a bite of chicken under the table. Later, when you're watching the news, you say to Rose

Anne: "Dr. Jackson's gonna take another look at me tomorrow. Gotta be over to his office at 8. So don't bother to cook breakfast."

"How could you not tell me about this?" She thumps her magazine against her knee.

"There's nothing to worry about; it's precautionary."

"You son of a bitch. You're always doing this. Living your life on the edge like that. Saying 'screw you' to God."

You get up from the couch, and walk over. She's stiff when you put your arms around her; then she starts shaking.

"Now, stop that, Rose Anne. It's going to be nothing. Really."

"I told you to do something months ago when I found that thing," she says.

"Settle down. Doctors are just trying to pay for their fancy vacations. If I hadn't known you'd fuss, I'd have ignored the whole thing."

When you lie back down to finish the news, Champ jumps on the couch next to you. He trembles when he stretches alongside the length of you.

Rose Anne's face is an awful shade of white in the glaring fluorescent lights in Dr. Jackson's procedure room. You lie curled on your side like the nurse told you. It irritates you to have to pee so often. Goddamn doctors.

He strolls in, his white coat not even buttoned, pats you on the knee, smiles over at Rose Anne. He washes his hands and explains what he's going to do: cold numbing gel, an ultrasound probe in your rectum, then the nine biopsies. A spring-loaded needle makes dull clicks as he pricks the tissue. Afterward, Dr.

Jackson looks over at Rose Anne, then speaks to her as if you're not even there. "O.K. That's it."

"When will we know something?" She's hunched over, her crossed arms flattening her breasts and her hair pulled back with a rubber band.

"It takes a few days. I'll call after I talk to the pathologist. Til then, though, don't let yourself stew."

Your headache hurts like a nightmare. When you're home on the couch, Champ rests the awful jaw on your chest. All day long, you click the remote: the strange news of an election eighteen months away, Barney Fife acting the fool in *The Andy Griffith Show*, dark analyses of criminals in jail. An evaluation of the death penalty by people in their forties. Flip. Flip. Flip.

Off and on, you rub Champ's loose skin. Rose Anne lets him out to the backyard a few times, serves you sodas with a straw, and a turkey sandwich with fake mayonnaise. She used to make a real club sandwich, but now she cuts out the bacon and uses some fake stuff that's only virtue is its wetness. You long for the real thing, and a decent tomato—nowadays she can only get those pink rubber things from the chain grocery.

"Drive Champ over to the vet," you say to Rose Anne. "Today can be Lump Day." You laugh, but she doesn't. "Really, I'm fine. It won't take you but a few minutes to get Champ fixed up. We won't get a call from Dr. Jackson for days, I bet."

As soon as you hear the tail of her car bounce against the gutter of the driveway, the phone rings.

Dr. Jackson wants you to come to his office. He seems to give you a choice: cut you open, radiation implants, chemo that you don't understand. "Shit," you mutter. "I'll let you know. For one thing, I read that just about every man over 70 has prostate cancer; something else always kills 'em."

"That's not exactly what we're facing, Grady," he says. "You really shouldn't wait. You and your wife should come in and we can talk it through."

Dr. Jackson seems way too young to know, but you do need to know what this'll do to your sex life; there are a few things Rose Anne won't live without. "Maybe."

"I can give you something to read about your options . . . when you come in . . . say, Friday afternoon?"

The phone drops into its cradle with a dull rattle. You walk right over to the refrigerator and open the way-too-small jar of real mayonnaise Rose Anne keeps hidden for chicken salad when she has her girlfriends over. She thinks you don't know about it. You dip your finger in, get a big dollop, lick the tangy stuff, then shake the jar a little so she won't know. You go on back to the television.

After awhile, you hear her driving up. Champ walks in front of her.

"Dr. Jackson call?"

"What did the vet say?"

Her eyes tear up. "Not good." She touches the dog on the head as she releases him. The leash is silly, but it comforts her. If Champ decided to get away from her, he'd just bound off; he's that strong. Instead, he's docile until she frees him. He looks at you, then lumbers over to his stainless bowl. He whimpers as he sticks his snout into the hard kernels, opens his jaw a bit, but the brown pellets scatter on the linoleum.

"What'd the vet say?"

Deciding that a pet oncologist probably won't buy much time takes all afternoon.

You know something's got to be done, and it's up to you. If you'd had a mind to, if you'd taken the time off work, you're pretty sure Champ would've won every field trial he entered. Way too late for dreams like that now.

You've seen cancer ravage your best buddy Roland, seen Roland's first bravado. "Hey, who knows what a pancreas does anyway?" Roland said. "Might not even need it. Bet they just cut the bum tumor out, a little radiation, short round of chemo. Problem solved."

Roland told you this while trudging the fields that particular time without Sam. January last year—under gray skies. Last year was a bad year for birds—the previous summer was way too dry for those little quail babies to survive. You and Roland had hoped for a better season this year. Roland didn't even make it to the first of March.

To think: it would've been Roland you'd have made a pact with to avoid a bad end in case the wives couldn't take you out. It would've been Roland you'd have gone to about Dr. Jackson, Roland you would've trusted. Instead, Roland first lost his bravado, then lost even denial till finally, when you and Rose Anne visited him last, Roland's eyes never left his wife, as if he was some abused child with the CPS people hanging around. He became the worst kind of sissy—one who didn't even realize he *was* a sissy. "That's not for me," you said to Rose Anne. "I'd want out."

Rose Anne clutched the door handle. "It's wrong to play God, Grady. Sinful."

She probably could never be talked into anything different. She fidgets with fate, but slyly—with vitamin supplements and cutting out eggs and eating blueberries three times a week, regular exercise and checkups. She cried all the way home from Roland's, softly as she'd done when they discovered they couldn't bear children.

Now Champ is afflicted; pain bringing on the sporadic trembling and watering eyes. Rose Anne nags: "Why doesn't Dr. Jackson *call*?" she says, then answers herself. "I guess every minute he *doesn't* call, the safer we are."

You watch Champ, and rub his belly, then the sloping ridge between his ears, evidence of his pedigree. You monitor his every meal; the vet said the tumor in his jaw will eventually make eating impossible. Rose Anne buys him canned food, and by Thursday night, Champ eats only that. On Friday morning, Champ yelps when you touch his snout even slightly. Something has to be done; the decision belongs to you.

You clean your shotgun with the gun oil and the little fabric square. Rose Anne walks through with the vacuum. "Will you clean my gun too? I want to go. I guess you're taking Champ? Or maybe he hurts too much?"

You let her join you at the ranch sometimes when the guys aren't around because her real talent is cooking up the birds. This time you don't want her to go, don't want her questioning you, or confronting you with a morality for which you no longer have the luxury. Still, she's the closest person to you, and she'd have to be told in any case. Something has to be done. "Give it to me."

With your thumb and forefinger, you pinch the metal hinge of the dog-box, and Champ steps out. He lifts his head, sniffs. His nails click on the metal floor of the truck. Once he would run so fast onto the ground you didn't even notice the clicking. You reach down and rub the bony head. He looks up at you with approval, follows while you retrieve your gun from the gun rack behind the headrest of the truck. He ignores Rose Anne.

"Come on, boy," you say. He runs ahead, and every so often pauses, looks over his shoulder.

The sun is bright, the air bracing-cold—a day made for bird hunting. Your boots rustle the grass as you walk. Rose Anne follows.

Champ freezes and lifts a front paw; his tail stands erect. You inch forward and the quail flush with a whirr. You hit two, reload. Rose Anne shoots, hits one.

Champ retrieves one limp bird and brings it to you. You let him hold it in his fleshy mouth for an extra moment. The second one flopped six feet away, you deposit it into your canvas shoulder bag, then reach to remove the dead one from Champ's mouth, tuck it away too. Champ ranges again across the uneven grass and stops in a hard dirt clearing, points to a cluster of low mesquite. His tail flutters; his form is something from *Gun Dog Journal.* You wish fervently you could live in this moment forever, wish that Roland were here to see Champ at his very best. Thank God Rose Anne at least is here to witness it.

Your shotgun bends the grass on which you set it. You walk up behind him as you have a hundred times, your movements slow, deliberate. Not a muscle of his moves. You pause two steps behind him.

Your pistol is slick and hard in its holster on your belt. You finger the cold trigger, know for sure you're doing the right thing, the kind thing. You step forward, near him, put the gun inches away from the little area between his perked ears—the little slope hiding the dog-brain less than the size of an egg; you must force the bullet in quickly, cleanly. A soft tick sounds as you pull the hammer back. Champ turns his head; you point the pistol up and away. For a moment your stares meet. His eyes are liquid brown, quizzical, and he trembles slightly, his body taut.

Champ returns his attention to the task at hand, lifts his nose to the scent only he can smell, and stiffens even more—anticipating the shotgun shot, the birds falling, his gallop toward their bloody carcasses. Your hand can't be made to lower the pistol to Champ's head, your fingers can't be made to pull the trigger. You can't go through with it. Now you're thankful Roland isn't here to see.

Rose Anne walks up behind, silent in suede lace-ups, tucks her dead quail into your canvas bag. She gently takes the pistol from your hand. "I'll do it," she whispers. Champ glances over again, then returns to his point.

You learn the meaning of the word 'reverberate' as the shot shakes the air around you, then dissipates. Little puffs of dust rise where Champ's body disturbs the ground.

With quivering fingers, you close the brown staring eyes. You carry his body to your vehicle. A ragged horse blanket serves as a shroud. If the edges are tucked in tight, maybe the buzzards won't come to the truck bed.

Rose Anne takes the canvas bag, and sets it next to Champ. Loads herself into the truck to drive to the campsite you and Roland used. Rose Anne hands over the birds. "Here, you clean these. I'll make us some lunch." From a grocery sack, she retrieves the fix-ins, stokes up a fire, then fries up the quail and some chicken breasts. She makes a real cream gravy, scraping the fried crumbs from the bottom of her iron skillet, but the smell nauseates.

The vet asks no questions when you take Champ to be cremated. His ashes came back in a little cedar box with a gold-toned lock and key. You intend to scatter them on the site of his last hunt. The air is sanctuary-still as you open the little box, but a harsh breeze comes up just as you begin to pour, and blows the gray particles up towards heaven. Rose Anne stands behind you, and touches your waist with her palm as you turn back to her.

Dust to Dust:
A Prescription

IT'S PROBABLY A good idea to practice being dead. Just lie in bed and close your eyes, turn your mind off. It takes training but ultimately the resulting habit is worth it because when you actually get to the dying, you know what to look for. You're prepared. Plus, practicing can calm you better than alcohol, better even than the typical enmeshment with TV or Internet Bridge or even social media if you happen to have friends. In the same way those things don't really acknowledge your existence, practicing being dead at least doesn't bandy about a false reassurance that you are a significant blob of protoplasm.

Way back when Jimmy Dale broke up with you, you might have rehearsed on the wooden floor of your bedroom instead of your bed. The physical discomfort helped clean your mind of extraneous thoughts of his hands on your skin in the backseat of his car behind the stadium. In college, the practicing needed to be out of the way of your dorm-mate's mess and anyway, everyone kept interrupting you. Finally though, once you get a job and your own place, your dead-training can return to the bed which is much more realistic. You might not want to confess your expertise to anyone at the church if you follow through with joining.

You definitely should continue practicing if that basal cell problem turns into melanoma. Training is absolutely required if you check the Internet for expectations. The letting-go part of the dead routine may be more challenging in that case. For example, if it's your first go-round with a melanoma, you may start fantasizing about wearing caftans instead of bikinis. After the third or fourth diseased mole, you'll have to concentrate to erase thoughts of looking like Frankenstein when naked if such an opportunity for nakedness should ever present itself. You could find yourself conjuring up such an experience, or even conjure a memory of Jimmy Dale. Such images can produce a severe disruption of focus.

Eventually, you'll need to practice an absence of fear, a state of being which can be difficult with your adrenaline pumping. The absence of hope can be nigh near impossible to achieve in such circumstances.

You may forget to practice for long periods of time. The primary reason for such forgetfulness could be denial, or even simple busyness. However, memory loss can also result from a flow of desire/satisfaction through your life: you want or even need something and somehow it just appears or occurs. Such as the Oriental rug for your living room or a Louis Vuitton purse or even membership at the country club. These things may come to you soon after your desire/need for them and then be followed hard on by the next lust or requirement. This can happen so regularly the closets become stuffed and the calendar becomes oppressive.

Until something new reminds you of dying, it might not even occur to you that nothingness could exist. For example, Susan Dale, who ended up married to Jimmy Dale, might experience a heart attack. She could be rushed to an emergency room nearby and meet her demise, leaving Jimmy with five motherless children and a beat-up Subaru. This event may prick your guilt because you are deeply relieved you didn't end up married to Jimmy Dale, but also terrify you because Susan Dale was only 50. She would miss everything, even seeing her own face in the faces of her grandchildren. Course, she wouldn't have missed Jimmy Dale.

The drama of this event may inspire you or depress you, but may also invigorate you, leading you to take up your practice more religiously. You might even join the Funeral Committee at that church, which would remind you that things usually happen to other people. You might offer to deliver your Wild Rice and Artichoke Casserole to the bereaved since it went over so well with the Dale children. Delivery of casseroles will solidify your practice of being dead, but neither delivery nor practice can fully prepare you for losing everything. Practice may make perfect, but it doesn't supplant the blank spot next to you in the bed. Nothing prepares you for that.

Extol Him Who Rides on the Clouds
2

Call me Magdalene.

Not Maggie. Not Meg. And certainly not Dolly, for God's sake.

Call me Magdalene. Let the syllables roll off your tongue. Slowly…slowly…

Let the connotation seep into your stomach, your very skeleton, your middle there.

Take a breath. Narrow your eyes. What do you want?

Think: do you *really* love your life? Your job…your grown children…your spouse?

Is what you have now really enough for you?

Take another breath.

Touch my cheek…my silver-sheathed breast…me.

Keep breathing now.

Hear the raging air blowing all around us. Feel the wind's unpredictability.

Sense the precipice beneath our toes. Smell the gift.

See how our bodies sway just before they're beyond choice?

How our chests cease to heave?

We fly for an instant, holding each other for an infinite moment of understanding.

See the puffs of dust rise in frilly clouds that our bones make

     as they crack on the sun-scorched earth.

Author's Note: Somebody famous said, "Real writers steal."

    I don't know if I'm real but I am certainly a thief. For example, I plagiarize the Bible, specifically Psalm 68. Plus I filch Magdalene from church tradition that is also in writing by some dead white guys who, in a hubris-soaked fit of calling right wrong, and wrong right, falsely accused her of prostitution. Also, I appropriate from another of God's creations: Melville's *Moby Dick*, a whale of a good story about the wrestling of evil with good. If you, Dear Reader, investigate for yourself these sources from which I gratefully steal what I am certain is now mine, you can also learn a lot about fishing.

Jericho

LOOK AROUND THE den that serves as sickroom in the house he bought for you. "Amends," he said, "for bad behavior." You can still recall that laugh. Making the house perfect took a whole year. Highland Park homes shift and crack in Texas soil; making it strong again took diligent foundation repair but now the house is full of light, serenity, the restoration of the elegant architecture so lusted for: solid, polished, hospitable. With red rugs and pale gray plaster walls. What any woman would long to possess.

You set your rings amid the chaos on the bedside table: morphine, half full glasses of water, useless canisters with calorie-rich shakes now flat and hot, wadded-up tissues, and pill boxes for every hour of the day. Your bargain is clear to you as you stare down at his body. You know he is dead because, when he gasped and you tried to connect with his gaze as you always had, he did not focus for even a moment. It was finished. The hospice nurse has already called the funeral home and across the room, she dumps the drugs into a bowl of bleach. You consider filching the morphine, but instead hand it to the nurse and she dumps that also. Nothing can make you feel any better although as you glance around the room, you suspect no one will believe anything you say about it. Everyone loves to give advice.

You wash his body with long gentle strokes and the caregiver helps put on the freshly pressed pajamas. You do not cry. Duty requires deliberate action. Once you are finished, as you replace your rings, you ask your sister-in-law for a very large glass of wine. It's worth a try.

When the funeral director arrives, he covers your husband's face and rolls him out on a stretcher on wheels that form an 'x' like the cross at church. Without deciding to, you stand up. Everyone rises: your children, his sisters, the pastor, your husband's best friend. Once you down the wine, you trudge up the stairs and fall into bed with your clothes still on. In the morning, and for months afterwards, your body aches because you have never moved in your sleep like normal people.

You do what you must and collapse at the end of each day in front of the television with dinner and Chardonnay until you are sure you will sleep. This lasts for thirty-three months. Friends stop asking how you are doing. You've been in the Grief Support Group too long. No one seems to understand that nothing makes you feel any better. The doctor offers you antidepressants. People who can't listen show up with books you have no concentration to read. Why can't anyone understand there is no help for this.

One day you awaken and you cannot bear the mess another minute. You gather up his clothes, his books, and all the accoutrements of his hobbies: the hunting guns, the camouflage pants, baseball hats. The lawyer tells you that you must move to someplace 'more manageable,' but the thought is impossible, overwhelming and exhausting beyond belief. Still, your children start haranguing and you arrange to do what you can toward the goal. The broker's name is Dodie and though she's older than you are, she still has her husband, is still a wife. She cannot change anything for the better.

In the Grief Support Group, they extol rituals, so you set some up for yourself. You read the Bible every morning and write feelings down, then burn them over the toilet. This does not work.

The record of your history with him is on every wall and the photographs torment like strobe lights at a party you didn't want to attend, so you pack the photos in a closet. You redo the den in which he died, which the hospice people insisted be his final sickroom. You recover the couch, replace the glass lamps with their taxidermy'd quail inside. You put up modern art and sell the bird dog painting he loved. You get a better television, find a place to buy wine by the case, then start feeling bad about it. Your therapist rolls her eyes.

You try moving your rings to your right hand but hastily return them to their correct place. Dodie offers house after house but there's always something wrong: not enough bedrooms, too expensive, not enough storage, not enough light. Nothing works; nothing makes you feel better.

Friends begin to worry, suggest traveling or taking up mahjong or going back to needlepoint. One even audaciously reminds you how lucky you are. You nod, you agree, you consider backhanding her. You decide to go to a spa.

The spa offers 'challenges' and you sign up for the zip line. Some kid instructs on how to use this experience to learn about yourself. You are harnessed and climb up the four-story tower, and try to trust the equipment. Although your terror is palpable, you stay focused to get to the platform on top where the wind blows. You white-knuckle the rail to stay upright; after a bit, it's livable. When it's your turn to hook onto the zip line, the kid says, "Just six inches of fear, then you get to fly. Better than sex!" He laughs and you think: a lot he knows. But you let go and it *is* a lot like flying, with only a too-thin wire between you and a calamitous collapse. The tension doesn't eradicate the words in your head: Alone Bereft Alone. The suitcase clatters as you unlock the door in the twilight and a sigh of relief escapes you. Your reliable, perfect space…silent. Thank God you're finished trying that.

The succor you've created for yourself begins to trouble you. So you redo your bedroom. Replace the king-sized bed with a queen. Change the dresser, replace the prints on the wall, add a television and a little cabinet for coffee and wine almost like in the movies. Now nights will be less cavernous. Surely it's progress. Surely.

Dodie calls with a house. "Checks every box," she says and when you tour it, you are forced to agree. But you can't make yourself put in an offer. At home, you look around: how can you leave this? This has been your solace and the walls like a moat protecting a fortress: safe, forecastable, secure with a time-stop-still quality.

Lent descends and you give up your nightcap. There's less now to shield you from the full-turned-empty. Somehow you're glad of the pain. A week into the liturgical season, you offer to buy the house Dodie found and now you are going to own two houses. You look at the advertisement for the new one over and over and over. The house is in a gated community designed for people with grandchildren and plans. Envisioning yourself there begins to make a bit of sense, even to elicit a dull appeal. As you stare at it, you turn your rings around and around and around.

The windows and archways from one room to the next in the house that your husband bought you have created a womb-like silence. You keep trying to work out how to own both houses, but it's impossible financially even if it wouldn't be so unwieldy. Even renting it makes no real sense. On the last day of the option period for the new one, your daughter calls to find out what you've decided. "I'd hate for you to get stuck, Mom."

After the closing, you stop by the jeweler and buy a sapphire ring with pave diamonds on the band. You slip it on your finger and gently set your wedding rings into the velvet box for the sapphire. You drop by the bank on the way home and lock the gray velvet into the safety deposit box. You can revisit your diamond and the plain platinum band whenever you want – peer at them, cry over them, even long for them – but you don't want to insure it any longer. You just can't afford that anymore.

The fall wind has blown leaves off the oaks in front of the house that he bought for you that will soon be no longer yours. The late sun is out. The half-bare trees force a seductive, dappled light onto the façade. A bit of fumbling is required to retrieve your keys from your frayed pocket. As you unlock the front door, you notice the door-face bricks are crumbling.

Ticking

EVERY DAY, WHEN she awoke, she started her pre-dawn prayers with apologies to God for making so many mistakes in her life. Such things as letting her mind wander off from her children's dramas or resenting her husband's purchases like the leather-handled hammer that cost $25 when they needed diapers for the baby so long ago.

She closed her prayers with the knowledge she was, after all, still alive and still lived in a home, and asked for help to get through the day.

After prayers, she tried to get her mind off her troubles by taking the dog Maddie for a walk. She would click the leash on Maddie's collar and head out the back door of the townhouse that was her home now that her circumstances were reduced. Being outside as the sun rose had its hazards. Sometimes she missed the dark pinecones on the path or sometimes even tripped. Every so often she forgot to refill the hummingbird feeder next to the back steps. But she tried very hard to be present to the burgeoning light and had come to enjoy hearing the mockingbirds mimic the other birds' expressions of themselves. She wanted to discover a measure of magnanimousness and serenity within herself.

Maddie always panted by the time she opened the townhouse door, as she looked forward to the one cup of coffee she allowed herself. She walked around her silent world, removed the orthotics from her old-lady shoes and, if it was humid outside, wipe her glasses of the moist haze that made worse her cataract-burdened vision.

No children's tales greeted her. The leather-handled hammer was long-discarded after Frank finally succumbed to cancer, and besides the sight had torn at her after he died. All these evidences of her inadequacy disquieted her with the eternal tick-tock of the watches and clocks that pretended to arrange everyone's lives.

Her cell phone rang in her pocket, slashing the quiet. It would be Bruce, her eldest, checking on her as he did at eight o'clock every morning. To verify that she was still alive.

He didn't have a clue.

The Thing to Know About Coffins: An Essay

If we think about it, any mother's womb is a kind of coffin: dark and tight and seemingly inescapable. For most of us, in that space we were entirely alone except for a mystical thump thump thump of a mythical person who eventually would be called Mother. Before that, of course, we did leave that increasingly tight repressive state.

For a good long while, it might've seemed we had escaped coffins altogether, or maybe that coffins didn't even really exist except in movies to titillate our fears. Such was a nice belief: that coffins existed for everyone else except us and that our coffin experience was behind us.

We become so sure of it, in fact, we don't even notice that biology keeps offering us living metaphors for coffins: sexual affection, marriage, then progeny. Most people don't even realize those offerings aren't exactly metaphors. We can get stuck in the idea that we are bullet-proof or infallible. Or else we are stuck with some idea that no walls exist that can enclose us – but that's because the walls haven't closed in yet.

One thing unfolds after another in the natural course of life, all coffins of various sorts. There is some choice along the way, but those choices can be hard for us to recognize since recognition takes courage and a certain amount of contemplation to realize they are whispering in our ear.

The various sorts of coffin walls can look a lot like a mortgage. At first, they can seem silk-smooth and pastel-soft because what we are moving into seems so grand and smells like new. But the vulnerability of being a human being results in suffocation as the newness disintegrates all around us like so many ugly snowmen.

Being a biological creative, subject to the elements, probably we will trade in the current coffin over and over again for a new one, thinking the new one will free us. Eventually the fact that the metaphor isn't a metaphor at all assaults each of us.

Ultimately, most of us begin trading down our coffins. This probably won't be much of a choice; any children will insist. A lot of us are no longer able to walk without a walker or a get around without a wheelchair. Eventually not even those help us move.

The coffin called the Independent Living Center becomes a shared room in some Assisted Living place that smells like pee. The resources from said previous coffins have evaporated. We are forced into a roommate who may not talk to us; we are forced into silence.

Finally, it dawns on some of us that the *real* coffin is actually our epidermis. We might have realized this when we were squeezed out of the mythical mother's womb, or maybe even when we were conceived. Being that biological creature, we forgot. We were believing lies perpetuated by the beauty of the world or perhaps by some malevolent force bent on distracting our consciousness. Yet, if we really consider the facts from our experiences, we know for certain we have left every coffin we ever found ourselves within. Like an unsubstantiated but entirely probable hope, it occurs to us that we might not even be biological creatures at all.

So, we wonder. We really do.

Acknowledgments

My gratitude to the following who have encouraged my work: Harold David Croan, Sue Pasmore, David Jauss, Doug Glover, Anne Stinson Crow, Rosamond Brown, Carrie Jane Bieda, Robin Underdahl, Elizabeth Hamilton, Libby Beach, Mary Jo Oliver, Wally Lamb, Mary Lessmann, Robin Hemley and Ben Fountain.

Also, my many thanks to the following journals for publishing stories in this collection:

Numero Cinq
"Extol Him Who Rides Upon the Clouds"
"Exercise in Memory"
"On the Occasions the Lula Sought an Answer from her Mother's Bible Concordance"

SLAB
"Indian Blanket"

Summerset Review
"Point. Click."

Between the Lines
"Because She Was Rich"
"Windows"

Blue Fifth Notebook
"Proof"

Steel Toe Review
"Big Bend"

Sleet
"Chad's Room"

On the Veranda
"Secrets that Lula Keeps from Her Grown Daughter Who Always Overreacts"

Love After 70, Wising Up Press
"The Prayer of Doreen Newton"

After the Pause
"Forms of Defiance 1"

Ocotillo Review
"Serious Concerns"

Straylight
"A Metafictional Reality: A Tale of Metaphysics"

Blue Lake Review

"Jericho"

The Esthetic Apostle
"Oral Fixation

ABOUT THE AUTHOR

Stories from Dallas native, Cynthia C. Sample, have appeared in *NumeroCinq, Summerset Review, Sleet, Blue Lake Review, Starlight Literary Journal* and others. She holds an M.F.A. in Fiction from Vermont College and a Ph.D. in finance from University of Texas at Dallas.

About the Press

Unsolicited Press is a Portland-based small publishing house that supports authors from all backgrounds. With a feminist attitude and a hunger for finding the best literature out there, the team is constantly striving to present voices from every crack in the world. The press has published award-winning authors and has had more than a dozen titles win awards.

Learn more at unsolicitedpress.com

Follow on Instagram and Twitter (@unsolicitedp)

CPSIA information can be obtained
at www.ICGtesting.com
Printed in the USA
LVHW030248120222
710801LV00003B/432